Beechwood Acres

Miriam's Journal

A Fruitful Vine

A Winding Path

A Joyous Heart

A Treasured Friendship

A Golden Sunbeam

Joy's Journal

Tall Cedars Homestead

Beechwood Acres

Miriam Joy, who now goes by the name Joy, was just a little girl in the "Miriam's Journal series." In Joy's Journal, she marries Kermit, moves first to Tall Cedars Homestead and then to Beechwood Acres.

Joy's Journal #2

Beechwood Acres

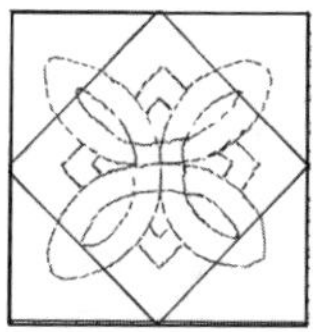

Carrie Bender

Masthof Press
219 Mill Road
Morgantown, PA 19543-9516

BEECHWOOD ACRES

Cover artwork
by Julie Stauffer Martin, Ephrata, Pa.

+ + + + +

Sketches in text
by Julie Stauffer Martin

Library of Congress Control Number: 2003100071
International Standard Book Number: 1-930353-57-X

Published 2003
Masthof Press
219 Mill Road
Morgantown, PA 19543-9516

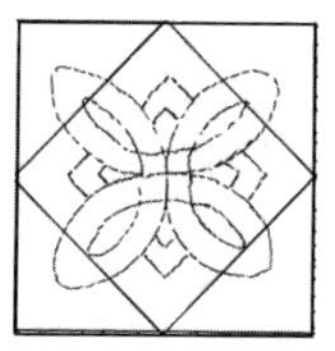

This story is fiction.

Any resemblence to persons living
or dead is purely coincidental.

Contents

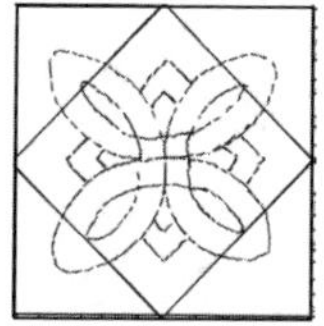

Part One

Spring at Beechwood Acres

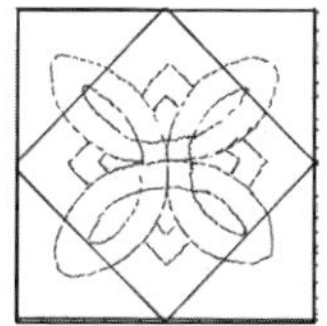

March 10

My husband Kermit and I arrived here at our Beechwood Acres farm three days ago and are still getting settled in. It's quite different from Tall Cedars Homestead where we spent the first one and one-quarter years of our married life, even though it's not that far away and still in Montana. Tall Cedars Homestead was a cattle farm with an experienced "cowboy" named Chuck living in a bunkhouse on the farm, and the "wild" mountain country all around us. It was a bit rugged and isolated, but we were happy there and wished we wouldn't have had to move out of our cabin home.

Beechwood Acres is more like the farms in Pennsylvania where I grew up. The three-story grey stone farmhouse has a large L-shaped porch on two sides with a wooden railing around it and a good-sized balcony above.

A wisteria vine crawling along the front porch roof will be spectacular when it blooms in May. We put up a wooden porch swing that we bought at an auction. It will be a lovely spot when the lavender wisteria clusters are blooming. There are plenty of trees all around, too, and that helps us to feel at home. A rocky, meandering stream flows through the meadow, and the old stone bank barn looks as though it could weather a few more generations. A pond and even a row of gnarled old apple and pear trees and some newer fruit trees, make me feel at home. Between the house and the meadow is a spacious (although twig-littered) lawn dotted with beech and elm trees. The beech trees are probably what gave the farm its name—Beechwood Acres. A blue spruce tree at each corner gives the yard a touch of distinction and color; the other trees do not have leaves yet. Beside the wide front steps are two interesting-looking stone urns that will make excellent geranium planters after the danger of frost passes.

Last evening Kermit and I explored our place a bit more, and I think we'll be able to make ourselves at home here. Chirping robins were hopping about, spring peepers were singing down in the hollow, and red-winged blackbirds were calling from the fields. On the south slope of the barn hill I even found a few dandelions blooming.

Ya well, Kermit will soon be in for supper, but I'll take the time to copy an inspirational verse.

> **Golden Gem for today:** *The manna of one day was corrupt when the next day came. We must have fresh grace every day from Heaven, and we can obtain it only in direct waiting upon God Himself.*

March 12

The snow has disappeared and the ground is fit for working. Kermit will soon start to plow the fields, and turn the sod to be cultivated for another year's crops. We know there's still a chance of more snow at this time of the year, but it won't hurt the plowed fields. I'm already getting spring fever as I look forward to the time when the trees are overflowing with green leaves, the birds singing joyously and building nests, and the wildflowers blooming. Kermit brought in a nice bouquet of crocuses this morning—how thoughtful of him! He knows I like flowers. We are enjoying our time of being alone again, without Treva and Jared, our *Maad* and *Gnecht* (hired help). They are finishing their school term at home with their parents and will come again in May. We love to have them because they're almost like a brother and sister to us, but we also appreciate being alone as well. We'll be plenty busy soon, though, and could hardly do without them; this is a large farm and we plan to raise produce.

Now I'll describe the interior of our house, starting with the kitchen. It's a big one with old-fashioned knotty pine cabinets and an antique built-in corner cupboard with lots of little glass windowpanes in its doors. There's an antique built-in jelly cupboard, too. With so much room, we'll be able to stretch out our new table with all the extra leaves in—twenty feet—for company dinners. There is a set of double folding doors over to the *Sitzschtubb* (sitting room) and a set from the *Sitzschtubb* to the *Commar* (downstairs bedroom). When they are opened, it will make a large room for church services. This place was Amish-owned two years ago, so it comes in handy now.

The *Sitzschtubb* has old-fashioned dark wainscoting, but above that is lovely new pale yellow-flowered vinyl wall covering. The parlor has the same wainscoting, but there is blue-flowered paneling on the upper half and new ceiling tiles. The *Commar* has also been redone with pink and green vinyl wall covering. Mom Mullet thought I was lucky to be able to have everything so nice. I feel the same way, even though I know it's only temporary.

It's a humbling but awesome feeling to be starting a home of our own. Kermit said that we want to have a Christian home that will be a beacon of light to others. It is our goal to live humble, God-fearing lives that bring honor and glory to God.

> **Golden Gem for today:** *Pride makes faith impossible. How can ye believe who receive glory from one another? Faith and humility are rooted together. We can never have more of true faith than we have of true humility.*

March 14

Kermit bought two more workhorses at a sale and began plowing. I saw flocks of seagulls following him like clouds. Mom and Pop Mullet were here for dinner today and brought a new gas stove for us to use while we're here. Pop helped to set it up, and now the kitchen looks so cozy. They think that some of the remodeling in the other rooms, although not too modern, seems more like English houses and advised us to use those rooms as little as possible. Oh, well, I guess there won't really be a need for them, except maybe the parlor when we get company.

Mom built up the fire in the stove and made a kettle-full of chicken corn soup for dinner. She had brought along a loaf of her delicious whole-wheat bread. Somehow, my whole-wheat bread never gets as light and delicious as hers. I guess I need more practice.

They also brought my treadle sewing machine, and after they left I hemmed a blue-and-white-checkered gingham cover for it, and then made a new kitchen curtain for the window above my sink. The one that was there was a bit too lacy and frilly to suit me.

Mom (bless her heart) brought my houseplants, too, and they sure add a homey touch to our kitchen. I placed a Rex begonia on a doily on the sewing machine, a lovely green-vining ivy in a hanging basket by the double windows, and several blooming geraniums on the windowsills. My blue-flowered ceramic canister set on the kitchen counter was a wedding gift from Rudy and Barbianne, and it gives the kitchen a special touch, making it seem more like my own. It wasn't until mid-afternoon that I thought of bringing in the mail, and then I had a nice surprise—a friendly letter from Rachel and Ben. She had enclosed a sheet entitled, "Roses Have Thorns." I thought it worthwhile, so I'll copy it here.

Roses Have Thorns

by Merry Mary Yoder

It is almost impossible to cut and arrange a bouquet of roses without collecting a few scratches and pricks from the thorns. When the bouquet is finished, some will admire the beauty and thank God for it; others will only curse the thorns.

A Christian marriage is much like a bouquet of roses. Individuals often are scratched and bruised. Too many cry over the hurts and never see the beauty.

Thorns left under the skin will fester into an ugly wound; they need to be removed promptly. When members of my family hurt me, I'd better face it honestly. If I deserved it, I'll need to admit it and ask forgiveness from that person. However, when I'm not guilty, I'll need to talk to God; ask Him to help me forgive and forget. This is like washing a tiny scratch with soap and water. It will heal quickly and leave no scar.

Each scratch, if treated immediately, will add to the enjoyment of the bouquet. When members of a family see each other growing sweeter through trials, they will see God's love in language they understand. This is the beauty of a Christian marriage: God's love glistening on the roses.

Are you enjoying your bouquet of roses (marriage), or are you more concerned about the thorns? Do you thank God for the beauty in your marriage, or does God hear only your complaints?

March 15

We did a lot of the spring work today. I keep thinking, wouldn't it be nice if we could own this farm and stay here twenty years or more!

I just finished washing and waxing the kitchen floor, and I'm sitting on the Boston rocker, waiting for the floor to dry. Now that I've added the finishing touches to our big kitchen, such as the homemade hooked rugs, crocheted potholders, homespun tablecloth, blue ceramic canister set, and wooden bread box, it looks even nicer and complements the antique built-in corner cupboard and knotty pine cabinets.

In the *Commar* (downstairs bedroom), our bedroom suite looks real handsome with the colorful Wedding Ring quilt on the bed and the braided rugs on the floor. In the *Sitzschtubb* (sitting room), we have another nice corner cupboard (made by a local craftsman) and an oak library table and settee. It's going to *shpeid* me (make me sorry) to move it all again when we have to leave Beechwood Acres, but I'll not worry about that yet. We'll enjoy this home while we're here.

We're looking for Ben and Rachel to stop in sometime; and now that I have the house all spick-and-span, I can hardly wait.

Our driving horse, Patsy, seems to be a bit lame, so Kermit wants to attend a horse sale tonight, thinking perhaps we can find another one that suits us. He asked if I wanted to go along, and if course I said I would—I've had never been to a horse sale before.

Golden Gem for today: *Regret nothing: breathe in the rich blessings of each new day and forget all that lies behind you. Man is so made that he can carry only the weight of twenty-four hours—no more.*

March 16

We went to the horse sale last evening. I've heard that a lot of girls attend horse sales regularly. It must be true, for I certainly wasn't the only one there.

Kermit and I sat together up in the grandstands—or whatever you call those seats with each row higher up than the one in front. We sat near the top, and it was quite interesting to watch the horses being led or ridden through the ring. First the big, heavy, chunky workhorses—Clydesdales, Percherons, Belgians, and others—then the up-headed driving horses—saddlebreds, Standardbreds, trotters, and pacers. The auctioneering and bidding was brisk, and although we stayed until late, we thought we would have to go home without a horse because none seemed to be just right for us, including the price. Of course, there were a lot we would have wanted, but the prices were sky high.

After the sale, Kermit talked with one of the jockeys who offered to send one of his horses just for us to try—we can have him on trial for two weeks, and then if he doesn't suit us, we can send him back without any charge. If we want him, the price is $2500 which sounds reasonable.

Our new horse arrived this morning—a big, up-headed bay gelding. Kermit hitched him to the two-wheeled cart and we took him for a spin to see what he's like. To make a long story short, he balked for us and we decided not to fool around with him, and sent him right back. I'm so glad we had him "on trial." Tonight Kermit led Patsy out of the stall, and her lameness seems much improved—hurrah! We probably won't need another horse after all.

> ***Golden Gem for today:*** *Give us our daily bread, O Saviour, Who art the bread of life, evermore nourish and strengthen our fainting souls by imparting to them Thyself.*

March 17

Sitting here at the west window I can see one of the most spectacular sunsets I've ever seen—a blending of reds and pinks and blues and even purple. The air is ringing with the sweet melody of a robin singing his evening vespers from the branch of a beech tree. A pair of song sparrows are checking out the old wren house on the fence, probably beginning to think of building a nest. We already like living here; it feels like home now and—"Be it ever so humble, there's no place like home!" I'll take the time to copy a poem I read.

Sharing

by Elaine V. Emans

Sharing begins with a host of little things;
A poem read, the rising of the sun
Across a lake, telling how some bird sings,
Climbing a hill together for the fun
Of standing side by side upon its crest,
Giving a gift, bringing good news, for it
Is better shared, and laughter shared is best.

Day in, day out, and slowly, bit by bit,
Sharing begins unconsciously with no
Thought of return except another's pleasure . . .
But mark how often it's been known to grow
Until the sharing of the heart's dear treasure
Is so compelling two become aware
How true their love is by their need to share.

I'll have to stop writing for now, since Kermit's coming in from the field with the horses.

March 18 (Sunday)

Springtime must be the loveliest time of year, with its promise of awakening of nature—birds, wildlife, growing things, balmy weather. There's the fragrance and sweetness of blooming hyacinths, the moist black earth where green things are pushing through, the robins serenading us from the apple tree by the garden. There isn't much that can surpass the beauty of the miracles of springtime with its indescribable delights to the senses. I can hardly wait until May, when the wonders of springtime will be at their peak.

Time seems to fly when one is busy and happy. Tonight Kermit and I found the time to explore the meadow and the woodland behind our place, following the meandering stream. We saw a small island with an old range shelter plunked down in the middle of it—a rather strange place for a chicken house to be—perhaps high water carried it there. A narrow rivulet of water flowed on each side of the island—narrow enough to step right over onto the island had we taken the time.

Some distance further, we came to a road with a little bridge crossing the creek, and on the other side was a little green-shuttered house with a boxwood hedge growing all around it. We decided to knock on the door—perhaps friendly people lived there.

The elderly, white-haired man who came to the door had a kind face—a downright friendly expression—and he opened the door wide and invited us inside. He was joined by his twinkly-eyed, silver-haired wife, who introduced themselves as Mirabelle and Hal Oleson. She, too, invited us to come in, and so we did, glad to find the Olesons such friendly folks.

Mirabelle has a doll collection which she showed me—a doll for just about every country, and each one dressed in a different costume! It was something to see—little Emily would have loved them! But, of course, they're valuable dolls and not for children to play with. Hal teased Mirabelle about being in her second childhood—playing with dolls—but she tossed it right back, telling us that he takes as much of an interest in the dolls as she does.

They are a dear, old-fashioned couple, and I'm glad we didn't pass by without stopping. They told us that they had planned to go for a walk to visit old Mr. Bradford who lives in the mansion on the hill. It was about a half-mile out the road.

We decided to join the Olesons and were delighted for the opportunity to get to know another one of our neighbors, and Mr. Bradford was just as delighted to have company. He's at least ten years older than the Olesons, but his mind is still keen and he's quite an interesting character. He owns at least half a dozen big, healthy-looking cats with soft, luxurious fur. One was sitting on the sofa, another on a hassock, one was lying on the piano seat, and several were sprawled on the rug in front of the fireplace. He also has a dog—a purebred collie who just had a litter of pups that aren't purebreds, much to the old man's displeasure. He asked us if we would take one of the pups, and Kermit said we would, so Mr. Bradford is going to bring one over in a week or so. His house is elegant, and he has a housekeeper and a gardener, so it appears as if he is well-to-do. He used to be (or still is) an artist. We enjoyed the visits with the Olesons and Mr. Bradford. It will be good to have such friendly neighbors.

Kermit's outside at the moment, checking the stock, so I'll take the time to copy an inspirational verse.

Love Is:

- *a note of appreciation*
- *an unexpected rose*
- *an open line of communication*
- *an opened door*
- *a helping hand with the housework*
- *a look in the eye*
- *a touch*
- *support and encouragement*
- *an understanding smile*
- *a soft answer*
- *a giving heart*

March 19

We had a welcome visit from friends tonight—neighbors from our Tall Cedars Homestead days—Jill and Wynn, the newlyweds, and Jill's grandparents, Art and Delphine! We sure appreciated their visit as they told us about the old neighborhood.

We took them on a tour of our Beechwood Acres farm and they agreed that it was a fine place to live. Jill wants me to make her a quilt whenever I find the time—a Wedding Ring quilt just like mine. I told her that it will probably not be before next winter, and that was okay with her. We talked about our families, and Delphine mentioned that she's hoping to have a great-grandchild sometime.

Jill retorted, "Don't look at me—we're not planning to start a family for at least five years."

Imagine someone not wanting a baby! That doesn't seem quite fair to couples like us who are longing for the chance. Oh, well, good things sometimes take time, at least for some people.

Tonight Kermit and I went for a walk under the starry skies. We miss the tall cedar trees at the end of the driveway at Tall Cedars Homestead and long to hear the soothing sound of the wind sighing through their branches. But here there are beech trees, the pond, the big lawn, and already we're putting down roots here. Will we ever own a place of our own, where we don't have to think of moving in a year or so?

Here's a poem for Kermit:

I love you for your gentleness
And for your faith in me
And all the goodness that you have
Inspired me to be.
I love you for the confidence
You willingly bestow,
But so much more because you are
The sweetest one I know.
- Author unknown

March 20

More visitors today: Kermit's mom, his sister Stephanie, and her little son Hunter. They too think we have a very nice place to live. Hunter ran all over the farm, following Kermit wherever he went, wanting to look at all the animals, and asking questions. When they were ready to leave, Hunter begged to stay. Stephanie gave him permission to stay until after supper, when her husband Kal could pick him up.

Hunter was one happy boy. First he played with the cats, but they soon fled for their lives (or so they thought), much to his disappointment. Next he chased the banties until they flew up to the barn rafters, squawking and cackling for mercy. After that, he asked to ride a horse and Kermit sat him up on Dick's broad back. His eyes got big, and he was soon ready to get off.

When Kermit was ready to milk the cow, Hunter wondered what the cow's udder was for. When Kermit told him that's where our milk comes from, Hunter thought he was kidding.

So Kermit got the tin cup and milked it full of foamy milk and handed it to Hunter. He sure was astonished! Kermit told him he could drink it, but I suppose he didn't quite believe it really was milk, so we told him to pour it in the cats' dish. He said it must be magic—he hadn't known that milk comes from cows.

Next, Hunter wanted a buggy ride. Kermit didn't think he had the time to give him one, so I hitched Patsy to the cart and we went for a drive. Hunter loved it, but I soon noticed that his head was nodding; soon he was leaning against me on the seat—fast asleep. I put his head down on my lap and we headed for home. It was then that we met an English farmer on a skid loader, and poor Patsy was badly frightened—acting as though she had never seen one before. Like a flash, we went up over the low bank—bumpity, bumpity, bump—nearly upsetting the cart! Hunter slept right through the bouncing—I'm glad his mother didn't see that!

> ***Golden Gem for today:*** *Faith in a "prayer-hearing God" will make a prayer-loving Christian.*

March 25 (Sunday)

Today Mr. Bradford brought the puppy he had promised us. He's a cute tawny and gold ball of fluff, so we named him Fluffy. We invited the old man to stay for dinner and he accepted, saying that his housekeeper was laid up with lumbago and he was doing his own cooking these days. We had fried chicken, mashed potatoes, peas, and raisin pie. Mr. Bradford thought the meal was fit for a king, or at least he pretended to think so. He's a very interesting conversationalist, and his mind is still as keen as a young man's. His wife was a schoolteacher, so he had a lot of stories to tell about her experiences. He told us that his grandfather used to work on this very farm and that he painted a picture of this place long ago and would like to paint another one sometime. That sure would be interesting to see.

Tonight Kermit gave me a paraphrase of Proverbs 31 that he copied from a magazine. He made a few changes and adaptations. I'll copy it here.

- *Who can find a faithful husband? For his price is far above that of a "dream horse" or even a prosperous farm.*
- *The heart of his wife doth safely trust in him, whether he is at a horse sale, or comes home late from a farm sale.*
- *He tries to do the best for her and his family as long as he lives.*
- *He learns to use the tools of his trade and isn't afraid of a hard day's work.*
- *He is knowledgeable about church affairs and uses this for the family's enrichment.*
- *He rises early in the morning for his devotions and asks for wisdom for his daily tasks.*
- *He considers investments carefully and buys a home, or property, or business with an eye toward the future.*
- *He watches his health and gets the sort of exercise he needs to stay physically fit.*
- *His work is of good quality even if he has to put in extra hours to make it that way.*
- *He doesn't neglect his home, and he attends barn raisings and frolics.*
- *He is concerned about his neighbors and tries to help those who are in need.*
- *He isn't afraid of difficult times because he has learned to trust God and has done what he could to provide for the family.*
- *He nourishes himself and his family both physically and spiritually.*
- *His wife is well thought of in their community because he never belittles her.*
- *He has a hobby that is relaxing and worthwhile.*
- *He is strong and honorable and is a happy person, easy to live with.*
- *His conversation is wide and uplifting—in fact, he makes it a rule of his life to speak kindly.*
- *He is interested in all things that concern his family and is not lazy or indifferent.*
- *His children love him and admire him, and his wife is proud of him*

and says, "Many men have succeeded in this world, but you are the best of them all—if I had it to do over again, I would still marry you."

- *Flattery is deceitful, and good looks is only on the surface, but a man who loves and fears God shall be truly praised.*
- *This sort of man deserves to be treated like a king, for his life proves that what he believes is real.*

I had to smile at the changes he had made, but I thought they were quite appropriate. I'm truly thankful that he has proved himself trustworthy, and that my heart can safely trust in him.

April 16

Mirabelle Oleson stopped in today and asked if I wanted to go along to visit a friend of hers who recently had surgery. I quickly donned a clean apron and *Kapp*, and went along. I certainly was glad I went, for the friend of hers was none other than Mrs. Elegant, owner of our Beechwood Acres farm! She was so glad to see us and said we brightened up her day. We hadn't been there long when a car drove in. I could hardly believe my eyes—it was little Emily, whom we baby-sat while living at Tall Cedars Homestead, and her mother. She brought her little pet ferret, Mini, that had once belonged to Mrs. Elegant. That ferret would probably not be alive today if Mrs. Elegant hadn't paid for the surgery it needed.

When Emily saw me, she rushed over and hugged me, and it made me realize anew how much I had missed the little "sunshine of our home." She is such a sweet and precious little girl.

When I came home, I discovered that Fluffy had dug out the row of geraniums that I had planted this morning. Grrrr! They weren't damaged too much, so I repotted them. I plan to teach the puppy manners before I plant them again. Frost is predicted for tomorrow morning, so I suppose it was too early to plant them outside anyway.

I took Fluffy for a short walk tonight, down to the stream. We saw a bunny bounding away in a thicket, a muskrat diving into the water, and the frogs jumping. Such an interesting world for an eager puppy to explore, and soon he will have a heyday chasing after these things. Kermit joined us when he came in from the field, and then we sat awhile on the porch swing since it was a crisp, moonlit evening. Soon it will be corn-planting time, and he will be busier than ever.

I had a letter from Mom today, and she included a verse:

Virtue is worth more than beauty or wit;
In dark days—through old age—it comfortably fits.
Oh, seek to develop its form and its love
Until you are safely abiding above.

May 6 (Sunday)

Rachel and Ben were here today and Rachel gave me a clipping entitled "Ten Commandments For Married Couples":

1. Thou shalt make Christ the Head of thy home. (Keep thy home on the rock of Jesus Christ and it shall stand in times of storm.)

2. Thou shalt readily forgive and overlook thy mate's faults and mistakes. (Be ye kind, tenderhearted, forgiving one another, loving one another.)

3. Thou shalt obey the Golden Rule. (Do unto others as you would have others do unto you.)

4. Thou shalt not let the sun go down upon thy wrath. (Apologize, ask forgiveness, pray together.)

5. Thou shalt compliment thy mate each day. (Focusing your attention on your mate's better qualities will generate more of the qualities you compliment.)

6. Thou shalt never criticize nor belittle thy mate. (Do away with impatience, worry, nagging, and jealousy.)

7. Thou shalt be more concerned with giving than getting. (Withhold nothing except by mutual consent, and for God's glory. Read 1 Corinthians 7.)

8. Thou shalt take time for love and companionship. (Build up your love by words and acts of appreciation for each other.)

9. Thou shalt take the time for wholesome recreation and worthwhile experiences. (Keep a sense of humor and learn to laugh at yourselves.)

10. Thou shalt give Christ first place in thy home. (Take time for daily Bible reading and prayer.)

May 7

There is a crawl space under the east part of the house where we recently discovered that a family of skunks had made their home. Several times as we headed for the barn early in the morning, we saw either Mr. or Mrs. Skunk hurrying home after a night of foraging, then disappearing into the crawl space.

This morning we overslept a bit, and when we headed for the barn, the sun was already lighting up the eastern sky. By the early morning light we saw not one, but two of the handsome black and white creatures ambling slowly but purposefully towards their home. Kermit quietly slipped back into the house and got his shotgun. Bang! Bang! Both lay dead. Skunks are beneficial to farmers and ranchers (they eat grubs and beetles) but are not welcome under our kitchen. Besides, the skunk population around here is too high anyway. I was surprised that those dead skunks didn't release some of their scent, but Kermit said that if death is instantaneous, they don't.

Later, as we were eating breakfast, we heard a mewing sound—it sounded as though it was just under the table. Right away we knew what it was—baby skunks! Kermit went into the basement and opened the sliding panel that gives access to the crawl space. There in a nest of dried leaves he found two squirming little black and white striped babies, less than three inches long, not counting their plumes of tails. I thought they were so cute and asked Kermit if I could keep them for pets. He was amused, but said I could. I put them in a box of straw behind the stove and fed them milk with a medicine dropper every two hours. They seem to like it.

May 11

For three days the baby skunks have been thriving on my care, and I named them Scamp and Scruff, for I'd heard that skunks make adorable pets and can be deodorized.

Kermit's sister Stephanie stopped in today and asked if I could watch Hunter for a few hours while she went to the dentist. I said I'd be glad to. Hunter was so fascinated by those little skunks—he held them and cuddled them, and after awhile he asked if he could take them outside on the lawn to play with them. I said he could. A few minutes later he came rushing back into the house, yelling at the top of his lungs.

Oh, no! Our puppy, Fluffy, had snatched up those little skunks and made short work of them. Now I had the job of trying to calm and comfort Hunter. I racked my brain trying to think of what he'd like to do that would help him forget. Kermit was in the barn and heard Hunter crying and came in to see what the commotion was all about. He took Hunter out to see the horses, and while they were gone I mixed some gingerbread dough. When Stephanie came to pick him up, Hunter was happily helping to cut out gingerbread men and sticking on raisins for eyes and buttons, and he didn't want to go with his mom.

May 15

Kermit and I went for a walk tonight and saw that the first of the corn he planted is already shooting up. With all that lovely weather we've been having, it sure didn't take long. My sweet corn in the garden is up, too, and the garden looks really nice. I started a tiny strawberry patch, so I hope we'll be able to stay here another year. If not, someone else will get the berries.

This really is a productive farm, and it's not in danger of being swallowed up by the urban sprawl as some of the farms back in Pennsylvania are. It's a pity to think of some of that beautiful, fertile farmland being covered with asphalt and concrete, the trees all cut down, the wildlife destroyed, the traffic on the roads getting heavier, the peace destroyed, and all signs of nature gone. Oh, well, there's plenty of room out here, and the farmland here is nice, too.

It's barefoot weather—over eighty degrees, and things are growing by leaps and bounds. The meadow grass is lush and green and dotted with buttercups. The fruit trees are in blossom, and the birds are sweetly singing.

May 17

The wisteria are blooming, so we spend as much time as we can sitting on the porch. The lavender-purple clusters are so beautiful. Tonight we had visitors. The Mullets spent the evening with us and they were able to enjoy the wisteria blossoms, too, while we had a good visit.

Pop was telling stories of his grandfather's day. His grandparents had a hard time keeping enough food on the table for their hungry, growing family, and there certainly were no store-bought extras or snacks.

Their main fruit was canned huckleberries and blueberries. In the summertime when the mulberries were ripe, sheets and tablecloths were spread under the trees, and the little boys would climb up into the trees and shake them as hard as they could. The sheets were picked up and the berries emptied into tubs and given to their mother to can. The children's hands and faces were as purple as the berries. They would harvest all the trees in the neighborhood, because the town people didn't bother with them. In fall there were bushels and bushels of fresh turnips, and these were cooked with potatoes at almost every meal.

There were no Sunday shoes—Pop's family wore the same shoes to church as at home, because they each had only one pair. Saturday evenings when the children were in bed, their mother would take a cloth and rub the bottom of the blackened furnace kettle with it, and then go along the whole row of shoes lined up on the bench, rubbing them with the same rag. The black from the furnace kettle would cover the worn and scuffed places and make the shoe nice and black. Next she would rub them with melted tallow, which made them soft and pliable, and even waterproof.

Nothing was wasted according to Pop; everything was saved and recycled if possible. Women and girls wore high-topped button shoes, with a whole row of buttons down the side that needed a special hook to open and close them. Sometimes the brothers (to tease the girls) would hide the shoe hook, resulting in squabbles and bantering until their father investigated and restored order.

Times were hard for everyone in those days, not just the farmers. City dwellers were hardest hit; the farmers could live off the land. Road walkers were common and hardly a week passed by that a man or boy didn't stop in and beg for work.

But the farmers had nothing to pay extra workers, except for a meal or two, so no one was sent away hungry, even if it was only mush, turnips, and mulberries they were served, or huckleberries.

I was amazed at the details that were handed down in Pop Mullet's storytelling. He recalled that every summer when the huckleberries were ripe, his grandfather's family planned an outing to go pick them. Two horses were hitched to the big, flat wagon and the whole family traveled to the mountain together for the day. It was a special occasion when a picnic lunch was packed, and a real outing was made of it. Sometimes cousins, uncles, and aunts, went on the same day, too, and then their picnic was something really special. There were ham sandwiches, red beet eggs, cherry and shoo-fly pies, lemonade, and brewed mint tea. Bags of hay and oats were put under the seat for the horses. It was an exciting time for the little ones (all who were old enough to help pick huckleberries).

The road up to the mountains was winding and narrow—there were no paved roads up there—and the way was rocky. Houses along the road were very small and poor-looking, hardly more than shacks, and old men (and some not so old) sat lazily on the ramshackle porches smoking pipes. Little ragged and barefoot children stood staring at the wagonload of people passing by.

On the other side of the railroad tracks at a grassy place where some large trees provided shade, the men unhitched the horses and tied them to the trees. Someone always stayed with the horses to guard them and picked berries close by to keep an eye on the wagons, because they had learned that their things, such as food and blankets, would be stolen if no one stayed there.

The rest of the group, Pop Mullet continued, spread out over the mountainside, staying within calling distance of each other so no one would get lost. When all of the buckets, boxes, and kettles were filled with berries, everyone returned to the wagons, and blankets and tablecloths were spread in the shade where they sat down to visit and eat. When the train passed, the engineer leaned out of the cab and waved his cap. The horses were fed their hay and oats and led to the spring for a drink of water. Then they were hitched back to the wagons and the trek homeward began, with everyone tired and happy, thinking of juicy huckleberry pies and cobblers, and fresh berry soup (*bruckle* soup) made with cold milk, bread, and berries.

Pop Mullet also said something I had never known before. In his grandfather's day, the old men and women (even some of the aged grandmothers who ought to have known better) smoked their pipes in the evenings after the work was done. They thought smoking was good for something or other and certainly didn't know that it was harmful to the body. Even then, some of the women had their ears pierced and wore earrings, although not the plain people. They had had it done when they were young and sowing wild oats, and later they were ashamed of such a vain thing as pierced ears. Mom Mullet said she supposed human nature was much the same then as it is today, but that the devil has more tools to work with nowadays, with all the modern inventions like radio, television, and bad things on computers.

After everyone left, Kermit and I sat on the porch and visited until late, with the stars twinkling in the dusky sky and night insects singing, and the grass becoming damp with dew.

> ***Golden Gem for today:*** *The church of Christ suffers more today from trusting in intellect, in sagacity, in culture, and in mental refinement than from anything else. The spirit of the world comes in and men seek by their wisdom and knowledge to help the gospel, and they rob it of its crucifixion mark.*

May 18

Happiness is:

- Sitting on the porch swing in the evening surrounded by lovely clusters of blooming wisteria.
- Having Rachel and Ben stop in for a friendly visit.
- Getting a welcome letter from the dear folks back home.
- Having a pair of bluebirds build a nest in the bluebird house that Kermit put up.

- Finding a bed of lily-of-the valley blooming behind the woodshed.
- Having my whole-wheat bread turn out just right and hearing Kermit say it's the best he's ever eaten.
- Going for a walk along the creek in the evening after the work is done.
- Seeing Kermit's welcoming smile when he comes in from the field.

May 23

Our *Maad* and *Gnecht*, Treva and Jared Miller, have arrived and already they fit in like family. If only Emily Simmons could have come along! I think I miss her more now than I did at first—she also seemed like one of the family when we baby-sat her while we lived at Tall Cedars Homestead, and her mother went to her job. Emily was such a sweet little girl!

We're having real summer weather now and the weeds are rapidly growing, so Kermit is relieved that our helpers have arrived. They'll have to spend a lot of time out in the fields transplanting and hoeing, but Treva says she prefers that to working in the house. That suits me fine, because I enjoy doing my own housework and cooking.

But today we spent most of the day working outside, laying plastic for the watermelons. It was a cool, breezy day, just right for working outside. Treva and Jared sure can keep things lively. The field at the back end of the farm close to the creek is a good one for watermelons, for the soil is a bit on the sandy side, just what melons like. The birds sang sweetly from the other side of the creek, and we heard the chirr of a hawk.

The field is near an island in the middle of the creek a little way up, and I hope we can picnic back there soon and explore the place. An old abandoned range shelter is in the middle of the island. I think it was probably carried there by flood waters sometime or other, or else someone towed it there to get it out of the way. It was probably used for housing pullets out on the range at one time; then when raising pullets that way became unprofitable, it was just simply forgotten.

Several times I thought I heard voices from that direction, but I suppose it must have been my imagination; I doubt if anyone would venture out hiking and exploring in such an out-of-the-way place, so far from a road and civilization. It's at least a half-mile from Hal and Mirabelle Oleson's place and a half-mile from the farm at the west end of our place.

> ***Golden Gem for today:*** *It is not the faith expressed in moments of prayer and exaltation God looks for, but the faith that lays immediately to rest the doubts of the day as they arise, that attacks and conquers the sense of limitation. "Ask and ye shall receive."*

May 24 (Ascension Day)

We attended church services at Ben and Rachel's on Sunday. I think that each time we attend, we're feeling more at home in this community. The church district was divided since we moved to Montana, so it was a change and took some time getting used to, with us attending the district on this side.

Today was Ascension Day, a day for enjoying the beauties of the creek and meadow. After Treva and I packed a picnic basket and Kermit and Jared got out their fishing poles and dug fish worms, we set out to explore the back meadow. We had never gone that far yet—only looked wistfully at the loveliness from the back fields while we were planting watermelons.

We started out early while the grass was still dewy and the meadowlands misty and fragrant with their morning sweetness. Wildflowers bloom in profusion back there, and the chorus of birdsong is indescribable. We passed the old range shelter on the island, leaving that until later to explore, and followed the creek until we came to a man-made dam, where the water rushed down over neatly laid rocks. Above that, where the water was deeper, appeared to be a good place for fishing, so Kermit and Jared settled down there. Treva and I explored some more, going on ahead to see the beauties that lay around the bend in the creek, then circled back to the island.

That old range shelter still intrigued me, because it looked as if someone had been there recently. It was boarded over on three sides, with the wire netting exposed only on the south side, where the wooden chicken-net-covered door was. A bit to one side lay a circle of rocks forming a little fireplace with a grate placed on top.

The grass looked trampled down around the doorway. I think Treva was as intrigued and curious as I was, for she suggested taking off our shoes and stockings and wading to the island.

We were about to do so when Jared hollered and cheered, and we saw him swinging a big fish on his line. We ran over to see it, and in the excitement of his catching the biggest fish he had ever caught, we forgot about the island. We stayed to watch until it was time for lunch; then we spread the tablecloth on the grass under a sycamore tree. Everyone enjoyed our ham and cheese sandwiches, with some fresh little red radishes from the garden, macaroni salad, a lemon pie, and the cake Treva had made and frosted. Jared could hardly stay away from his big fish swimming around in the little pond he had made by surrounding the inlet in the creek with rocks. He sure was one happy boy.

After lunch Hal and Mirabelle walked down to spend the afternoon with us. Hal was an avid fisherman and hunter, so he had a lot of interesting stories to tell, which sure fascinated Jared, and Kermit too. Mirabelle is a nature lover and had her binoculars along for bird watching.

We forgot all about exploring the island until we were back home. But next time we will, because the more I think about it, the more I'm sure we heard voices the day we were laying plastic for the watermelons. We saw the little fireplace and trampled path in the grass to the range shelter doorway. I keep thinking that maybe someone has temporarily set up housekeeping in it, or I guess it could have been some neighbor children playing there. But, really, there are no close neighbors here. I guess we'll have to wait to find out until next time.

It's after supper now, and Treva has offered to wash the dishes if I do the drying and putting them away. She is at it energetically now while singing heartily. She thinks it's a breeze doing dishes for only four people, compared to the big pile of dishes that the dozen at her home create. Kermit and Jared are setting up the badminton net, so we'll go join them in a few minutes.

May 26

I'm so excited about the letter I got in the mail today—a letter from Mom! It contains earth-shaking news that fills me with both anticipation and dread. I've always known that Pop was an "outsider" years ago, and that we never really had any contact with his relatives, but I hardly ever think about it.

Now Mom writes that my paternal great-grandmother, my father's grandmother, has contacted them and would like my permission to come and see me. It nearly takes my breath away, the suddenness of it, wondering what she is really like. Mom writes that she is a widow and seems to be a decent sort. She visited my parents and the family and is very eager to see me, too. I talked it over with Kermit and he says it is my decision, since he has no fear that she will influence me to her way of life, whatever it may be. It is so good to know that he trusts me implicitly—dear, kind Kermit! Now it is up to me—do I really want to meet her? Sometimes I feel like I'm all in a dither about it, then at other times I feel very calm and sure that it would be the thing to do. I know I must write an answer soon, but it won't be easy, either way. I must pray about it and ask God for guidance.

> ***Golden Gem for today:*** *Take all that happens as My planning. All is well. I have all prepared in My love. Let your heart sing.*

May 29

The peonies along the board fence are blooming, and the rows of spirea bushes along the old stone wall are adorned in clouds of bridal wreath blossoms. The path to the meadow is thick with forget-me-nots and other wildflowers. Kermit hung up a foursome of dried gourds with holes drilled into them, and a family of purple martin birds have set up housekeeping in them. Their cheerful warbling brings back sweet memories of my old childhood home, and cheers all our hearts. Even Jared takes a keen interest in them and keeps his BB gun handy to scare off the sparrows that chase away our martin birds.

Last night I finally composed myself to sit down and write that all-important letter to Mom. My answer was yes, the great-grandmother I've never seen or even knew I had is welcome to visit us and get acquainted. I am thankful for my heritage and always want to remain with "my" people where I belong, and have

no fear that any other way of life would tempt me. I've been counting all my rich blessings and thinking of the precious faith, and all that has been won and handed down by our forefathers. Never would I want to leave it for the transient luxuries of the world, or the pleasures of things that lead astray. But now comes the hard part—the suspense and waiting. I keep alternating between wishing she would write to say she won't come until fall, and wishing she would come at once, so that the suspense and waiting would be over. *Ach my!* Patience and serenity are sorely needed. *Fosset ihre salen mitt geduldt.*

May 31

Pop Mullet gave a cow to us the first week after we moved here. We named her Brindle even though she's not a brindle cow. She's not like our old Bossy that we had at Tall Cedars Homestead—she's simply the gentlest and tamest creature! She grazes contentedly in the lush green grass all day long, swishing her tail at the flies, and then gives gallons of creamy milk every day. (I'm trying to put that letter and thoughts of my great-grandmother out of my mind, so I'll write about anything else.)

Pop also sent one of his dry cows for us to pasture. This morning at milking time, neither of the cows came to the barn as they usually do, so I went after them. This was no hardship, because taking a walk in a meadow on a May morning is one of the most delightful tasks a person can do. The sweet breezes, the almost rapturous fragrance of dewy grass, earth, and growing things, stray blossoms floating down, birds sweetly singing, the gentle morning hush over everything, and the awesome beauty of nature, all make you think of the Creator.

I saw a rabbit hopping away, a woodchuck scurrying into its den, and two squirrels scampering up and down a tree. Close to the island and the dam where we had picnicked, I spied a rose-breasted grosbeak and was craning my neck to follow its flight up into a tree, when I was startled and brought back to my surroundings by the sound of voices in the direction of the island. To my amazement, I saw three children just outside the range shelter. The oldest one, a boy of perhaps eleven years old, was bending over a small fire in the rock fireplace, holding a frying pan and stirring something in it. A girl just smaller than the boy was throwing a handful of twigs on the fire.

Another boy about five years of age came out of the range shelter and called, "Boy, am I hungry! Can we have bread for breakfast?"

I was partly concealed behind a mulberry bush about thirty feet away and hadn't yet been noticed. The oldest boy told the little one that there wasn't any bread for breakfast, but there was plenty of fish, and maybe he could go to the store and get some bread today. Just a few minutes later the girl walked right by me, not ten feet away, and went over to the dam. She pulled a bottle of milk out of the creek above the dam, then ran back to the boys, again going past without seeing me standing behind the shrub.

The little boy had placed three tin mugs on a stump beside the range shelter, and the girl poured milk into all three. Next she arranged four foil pie plates on the makeshift table, and the boy dumped portions of fish onto each plate from the frying pan. Then all three sat cross-legged around the tree stump and began to eat.

Not wanting to interrupt their meal, I decided to first find the cows and then speak to the children on the way back. Way at the farthest end of the pasture in a little grove of trees, I found Brindle with Pop's dry cow, who had just freshened. By her side, a wobbly little calf teetered on its shaky legs, nuzzling its mother's side, trying to find nourishment. I thought better of trying to prod the new mother and her offspring into heading for the barn, but Brindle willingly complied. I had a walking stick and it didn't take much brandishing of it to keep her going.

Coming close to the island again, I saw that the children had finished their meal. The girl was kneeling by the creek, washing the plates and cups. The little boy was hopping across some stepping stones in the creek, heading for the bank, and the older one was already over there, gathering twigs.

I decided that now was the time to speak. "Hello!" I said cheerily. "Are you enjoying camping out here?"

The girl gave me a frightened look, then with a cry of dismay, dived for the door of the shelter and disappeared inside. The boys both yelped something, then quickly splashed across the creek and disappeared inside the range shelter, too, and pulled the door shut behind them.

Well, well! Apparently the children didn't want to be seen, but why not? Were they afraid I would disapprove of their camping on our rented land? I decided that the best thing to do would be to go home and tell Kermit about them. I didn't want to further frighten the children.

Later in the morning when Kermit went to bring the new mother and her calf, he crossed over the stepping stones to the island and peeked inside the range shelter. The children were nowhere to be seen, but there were three sleeping bags inside, and a big box in a corner. Two knapsacks were in another corner.

A round tin canister stood near the doorway, and the lid was partly off. Perhaps the children had left in a hurry. Inside the canister were packs of saltine crackers and a block of cheese, several apples, and a box of instant mashed potatoes. A crudely constructed shelf along the eaves contained three plates, mugs, and spoons. Kermit reported that everything was neat and homey looking. But now we are more curious than ever. Why are those children camping all alone in our meadow? Don't they have any parents to care for them? We aim to find out but haven't decided how to go about it yet—we don't want to frighten them more.

Ya well, this all helped to distract my mind from excessive fretting about our coming visitor. It's good to think about other things until I hear from my great-grandmother again.

> ***Golden Gem for today:*** *Rest, that is, cease all struggle. Gain a calm, strong confidence. Do not only rest in Me when the world's struggles prove too much and too many for you to bear or face alone. Rest in Me when you need perfect understanding and when you need the consciousness of tender, loving friendship.*

June 4

She's coming! I had another letter from Mom and my great-grandmother plans to be here in a week's time! I'm still in a daze and find it hard to believe. A thousand times a day I find myself wondering what she is like. Will she be wearing a sleeveless blouse and short shorts and wearing makeup? Will she look like a movie star or be a pleasant, comfortable grandmotherly type? Will she be in her eighties or in her nineties? Will she be snobbish or friendly? Will she have a reserved personality or be warm and outgoing? Will she scoff at our way of life or be enthused and supportive? The waiting is hard for me, and I almost wish she would simply have come without telling us about it beforehand. But maybe the shock would have been worse.

Kermit, Treva, and I spent most of the day hoeing in our produce field, and it was good for me to keep busy. I try to put it out of my mind, but find it impossible. Mirabelle Oleson came over tonight and she thinks it's all very wonderful that Great-grandmother is coming, and by her delight, my own enthusiasm was revived. I hope the time passes quickly. I had it on the tip of my tongue to tell Mirabelle about the children camping back in the meadow on the island, and at the last minute thought better of it. Maybe we had better solve the mystery first, and find out why they are so secretive and frightened. Kermit agreed that that would be best.

Tonight we sat under the old apple trees in the orchard, talking until the stars came out. Jared had gone swimming with the Mullet boys, and two of their girls had come over on the pony cart and took Treva for a ride, so we had the evening to ourselves. Kermit talked of his grandmother whom he never got to see and doesn't even have a picture—she died when he was just a toddler. What would it be like to get to see her now? He had another grandmother, too, of course, but she died when he was ten years old, so he doesn't remember much of her, either.

June 6

Jared and Treva spent yesterday hoeing between the rows of plastic in the watermelon patch. They, too, know about the children living in the range shelter on the island and decided to keep their eyes and ears open for any sign of them. Together they plotted and planned how they could find out more about them without frightening them away. They decided that when the dinner bell rang, they would pretend to be heading back to the house. Instead, after walking a certain distance together, Jared would slip off into the bushes, and Treva would continue on up to the house alone. Jared would backtrack through the bushes and hide somewhere nearby to see what he could find out. He instructed Treva to save some dinner for him, because he would be late.

Their plan worked really well, and Jared was able to sneak up to the shelter without being seen. The children had apparently sneaked away through the bushes and hadn't returned to the island yet, so Jared decided to enter the shelter. He hid behind the big box in the corner and peeked out through a knothole in the board. After awhile he heard voices and saw the children coming back along the creek. The girl was carrying a loaf of bread and the older boy carried a brown paper sack.

The little boy was saying, “I hope that boy and girl don’t come back to work in the field this afternoon. I don’t like when we have to hide and can’t be here. This is our home now.”

“But remember, we don’t own it,” the girl reminded him. “Besides, I think they’re nice people and wouldn’t make trouble for us. But you never know. They might report us to the police and our stepfather would come and get us in no time at all.”

“Never!” the older boy said vehemently. “I’m never going back to that mean man. He’s not our dad, and we’ll run away again if he finds us.”

“He can’t make us live with him, can he?” the little boy asked worriedly. “I don’t like it when he slaps me.” He began to whimper.

“Hush!” the girl said. “I don’t think he will find us. We’re doing very well living here alone. We have enough money to last a long time. We can buy our food at that nice little grocery store, and no one asks questions. Pop won’t find us here.”

The little boy ran off to gather twigs, then Jared heard the girl and boy talking together in low tones. The boy said worriedly, “I’m kind of concerned about the woman who saw us the other day, and about the boy and girl working in the field. I’m not sure that they didn’t get a glimpse of us sneaking away. What if they do notify the police? Maybe we should move away. I never thought anyone would find us way back here. If only that cow hadn’t had her calf back here.”

“I’m not really worried,” the girl replied. “I think they’re Amish, and they wouldn’t call the police. Besides, they seem like nice people and wouldn’t do anything to hurt us.” She added emphatically, “At least if they knew how mean our stepfather is, they would surely keep our secret. We aren’t making anyone any trouble at all back here. Come here, Billy,” she called. “Bring your twigs. We want to heat our soup and put the fire out before the boy and girl come back.”

Billy came splashing barefooted across the creek, carrying a small armload of twigs. “I’m glad we have a neat little house to live in,” he said happily. “Who put the little house here for us? How did they know we needed it?”

The older boy laughed. "You're funny, Billy. This used to be a chicken house. I don't know how it got here on this island, but we're sure glad it's here. Remember, Pop told us once that farmers used to have chickens living in little shelters out in the fields. In the daytime the chickens could roam all around in the field, scratching for bugs and worms, and at night they'd all go into the shelter to roost, and the farmer would come around at twilight and close the range shelter doors so that no foxes or opossums would sneak in and kill the chickens at night. They aren't used anymore nowadays, but we're mighty lucky this one's still in good shape."

"And we were lucky to find those boards you nailed on three sides," Billy added. "Now if it rains we won't get wet."

"Soup's hot," the girl announced. "Get the plates and cups, Chet."

By this time Jared was beginning to be a bit worried about how he would get out of the range shelter without being seen. What if the children would lie down on their sleeping bags after lunch, and he would be trapped inside. Or, worse yet, if they would see him and run off and be afraid to ever return. But his problem was solved when he noticed that there was a door (or way of escape) at the back end of the shelter. The chicken wire was loose there, and there was an opening in the boards. A loose board stood against this opening.

While the children were eating, their spoons clattering against the tin plates, Jared stealthily pushed back the loose board and crawled outside. He crossed the creek, being careful to stay behind the range shelter until he reached the bushes on the other side; then he crept through the bushes until he was around the bend. He came home just after we were done eating, but Treva had saved him a plateful of food.

Jared had some interesting things to tell us about what he had seen. Now it's up to us to decide what to do. Is it safe for three children to be spending the summer alone in the woods? What will happen to them when fall comes and it's time for school to start, and when the snows and icy winds of winter come? Is their stepfather's treatment of them really as bad as they made it sound? I hope we'll be given the wisdom to know what to do. We want to do what's best for the children, not necessarily what they think is best. At least it gives me something else to think about besides the upcoming visit of my great-grandmother. I think I'll copy an inspirational verse yet before Kermit and his helpers come in from the field.

> **Golden Gem for today:** *Guidance you are bound to have as you live more and more with Me. It follows without doubt. But these times are not times when you ask to be shown and led, they are times of feeling and realizing My Presence. Does the branch continually ask the Vine to supply it with sap? No, that comes naturally with the very union with the vine. "I am the true vine and ye are the branches."*

June 13

My great-grandmother Gertrude just left for home tonight after a two-day visit here. It was very interesting to get to know her, yet I breathed a sigh of relief when she left, for it was a strain on me to have her here. She is in her eighties, a dear old-fashioned grandmotherly type (I was so thankful for that) with a loveable personality, so I had nothing to complain about at all. But still, it was a strain. We spent a lot of time talking, mostly about my grandfather (her son). According to her, he was a very fine person. He was everything to her, her reason for living, she said, and when he was killed in a truck accident, it just broke her heart. He was not killed instantly, but lived and was conscious for several hours after the accident. She claims that he was a Christian (as is she) and had professed faith in God before he died.

My great-grandmother said that both she and her late husband came from sturdy stock, a lineage of fine, upright citizens. Her great-great-(I don't know how many greats) grandfather came to this country from Switzerland in the 1700s and arrived at Germantown, Pennsylvania. His daughter kept a journal, and that journal has been preserved and recopied, handed down from generation to generation, and a copy is now in her hands. She said it would be a very valuable piece if it were the original, but it is not. It has been copied from the original, except for wording things slightly differently, as people tend to talk differently in each century. Her own mother (my great-great-grandmother) was the last person to recopy the journal.

When I expressed interest in the journal, she promised to send it by certified mail to me if I would be sure to take very good care of it and send it back again by certified mail when I have read it. I hope she won't forget, because I am interested.

Now I will describe my great-grandmother's appearance. She was dressed very modestly, with curly white hair framing her round face. She is a small woman, but well-rounded, and wears gold-rimmed glasses similar to Mom's. She only recently found out about me and we intend to exchange letters regularly. She is hoping to have a great-great-grandchild sometime—*ya well*, I hope she gets her wish someday! I told her we would very much like to have a baby if it is God's will for us, and hope He will not withhold that blessing from us, because it is God who plans and directs our lives. She smiled and shook her head saying it's a nice thought, but she doesn't think that God works that way. I didn't contradict her; we each have our own opinion. We want to trust in God, whatever betides, and not become impatient and discontent of our lot in life.

We talked about her husband and their early life together. They were farmers, too, the first ten years of their married life. But when their only son was born, they left the farm and her husband got a job in town. She told me a lot of interesting things about my grandfather—about the scrapes he got into, and how he got out of them. Some of them were nothing to be proud of (in my opinion), but I guess he could do no wrong in her eyes. Maybe sometime I'll write them down, though.

All in all, we had a very good visit, and Kermit said that he was impressed by her. Now we're both eagerly awaiting the arrival of that old journal. Let's hope she doesn't forget it.

June 16

Happiness is:

- Having a bouquet of fragrant red rambler roses on the kitchen counter and breathing in their wonderful scent as I write.

- Picking a big bowl of luscious, red-ripe strawberries to eat with shortcake for supper.
- Getting a letter from Rachel and Ben and being able to rejoice with them in their hopes of the arrival of another baby in November, without my becoming envious.
- Sitting on the back porch in the evening, breathing in the fragrance of the new-mown hay and listening to the bob-whites call.
- Finishing a batch of strawberry jelly and sampling it with a piece of freshly baked homemade bread.
- Having Kermit's mom and sister Stephanie drop in unexpectedly for a visit in the evening.
- Being rid of a bad case of poison ivy acquired while pulling weeds behind the barn.
- Hearing the martin birds warbling and chirping from their gourd homes.
- Seeing Kermit's welcoming smile when I come back from a day of helping Mom Mullet with her berries.

> ***Golden Gem for today:*** *Seek diligently for something to be glad and thankful about in every happening, and soon no search will be required. The causes for joy and gratitude will spring to greet your loving heart.*

June 18

What lovely, rare June weather we're having! It's the month of blooming roses, ripe strawberries, delicious fresh hull peas, and other fresh garden goodies. This afternoon our interesting neighbor, Mr. Bradford, came with his easel and palette of paints and brushes and wanted to paint a picture of our Beechwood Acres farm. Kermit and Jared had gone over to Mr. Bradford's a few times to do yard work while his gardener was away on a trip. Hanging in his living room was a painting he did of this farm. Apparently, he often played in the orchard and spruce woods on this farm. Jared helped Mr. Bradford find a level spot to set up his easel with a good view of the farm and the spruce woods in the background.

Before supper, I went out to see his picture and to invite him to join us to eat. The painting was about three-fourths finished and he had done a very good job capturing the quaint, picturesque charm of the barn and the big windmill, with the blue sky for the background. Mr. Bradford brushed aside my praise and said that his talent is rusty and his hands don't cooperate as they did in the past.

He gladly accepted my invitation to supper, and I believe he really enjoyed it. He said it had been years since he had had fresh peas out of the garden and strawberry jam like his mother used to make. He had a lot of interesting things to tell about this neighborhood and our farm in the bygone days. After supper he went back to his painting, and just before twilight he came in with the picture and presented it to us as a gift. Kermit plans to make a frame for it, but I don't think we'll hang it on the wall for display—on the inside of a closet door would be better, or maybe we'll keep it in a drawer to look at every now and then. After we're perhaps living far away, it will be good to have a remembrance of this farm and Mr. Bradford.

Mirabelle Oleson stopped in a bit later and was amazed to find Mr. Bradford here; I guess she didn't think he could walk that far anymore. She offered to drive him home and I was glad, because we were concerned about his walking so far alone in the twilight. He claimed he's used to walking and loves it and has walked many miles in his time. But still, he's stooped and not as spry as he once was. Mirabelle loved the picture, too, and I think she was a bit envious. Maybe sometime he will paint one for her, too.

June 19

Every day when I go to the mailbox, I'm hoping for a package from Great-grandmother Gertrude, but so far I've been disappointed. If she would know what that old journal means to me, she would send it without delay. Treva and Jared have been busy hoeing in the watermelon patch between the rows of plastic. They are still very curious about the three children living in the range shelter and aim to find out all they can without frightening them away. Kermit and I are concerned about them, too, and wonder what we should do.

Yesterday Jared's curiosity got the better of him again and when Treva came in for dinner, he again backtracked through the bushes and hid behind the box in the corner of the range shelter. When the children came trooping back to prepare their lunch, he again eavesdropped while peeking through the knot-hole in the board.

The little boy came splashing across the creek to the island first. "Hurry up, Chet and Diane," he called. "Let's get the fire started so we can roast those doggies. I'm as hungry as a bear." He began to energetically gather twigs.

"I'll go for water from the spring after the fire's started," Chet, the older boy, said. "We'll be thirsty after eating hot dogs and buns."

Diane said, "Oh, no! We forgot to buy ketchup. Hot dogs won't be good without it."

The three children looked rather forlorn, but then Chet's face brightened. "I know! We have that tin can of tomato sauce we bought last time. We could use that as a substitute for ketchup. It's in the big box in the range shelter. I'll get it after I've gone for water. But first I'll cut sticks to spear the doggies with."

Jared said his heart was pounding hard; he figured Chet would probably find him hiding behind the box when he opened it. He crouched there in suspense while Chet went for the water, then cut long twig branches from the surrounding bushes.

Soon he was back. "Let's have those doggies, Billy," he said. "The fire's burning well now and we want to roast them before it dies down."

The three children squatted around the fire, holding their skewered hot dogs above the flame. "What would Pop say if he could see us now," Billy said, chuckling. "He probably thinks we're still doing lessons with Duffy. I'm glad he can't, for he'd be mad as a hornet."

Diane said, "I wonder if he put a notice in the paper that we've disappeared. If he did, we'd better be careful, or someone will be on our trail."

"He probably called the police," Chet said. "That is, if he came home at all before he left for Florida. He didn't know that Duffy broke her leg and that her sister came and took her to her home."

"Hey, wouldn't that be great!" Diane exclaimed. "I never thought of that happening. No one would know a thing about us leaving home. We'd be safe here for the summer, if that boy and girl hoeing in the field don't come snooping around here."

"But what will we do when fall comes and the weather gets cold?" Billy asked. "We'll freeze out here for sure."

"Don't worry," Chet said comfortingly. "We'll enjoy our freedom and camping out here, and something will be sure to turn up for us then. We're going fishing again this afternoon, you like that, don't you?"

"Sure," Billy replied. "But I'm tired of always having fish for breakfast. Couldn't we have some eggs instead?"

"I'm sorry, but that little grocery store doesn't carry eggs," Diane told him. "And we can't always have milk either, because it doesn't keep without being refrigerated and we can't go to the store every day. The clerk might get suspicious and start asking questions."

"Say!" Chet suddenly exclaimed. "Couldn't we somehow get eggs and milk from the farm where the boy and girl live? That would even be closer than going to the store."

"I don't see how we could do that without them asking us where we live," Diane said thoughtfully, shaking her head. "No, it wouldn't work. Hey, Chet, can you get that can of tomato sauce now? My doggie's ready."

Jared wasted no time. He quickly exited the rear entrance, disappeared into the bushes, and was soon back here in the kitchen bursting to tell us all he had learned. He thanked Treva for the heaping plateful she had saved for him, and tried to tell us all about it in between eating.

Kermit and I have decided that the best thing for us to do for now is to secretly keep an eye on the children, and as long as they seem happy and healthy, let them enjoy camping. Maybe we should invite them for a meal sometime and offer a supply of milk and eggs, if we could do it without frightening them. They seem to be nice children who probably don't have a mother, the way it sounds. Duffy is probably their caregiver, teacher, housekeeper, or governess, depending on how well-to-do the family is. We sure hope things will turn out all right for them.

Golden Gem for today: *"Ye are the salt of the earth; but if the salt have lost its savor, it is henceforth good for nothing, but to be cast out, and to be trodden underfoot of men." Only in very close contact is the keeping Power realized. That keeping Power which maintains the salt at its freshest and best also preserves from corruption that portion of the world in which I place it.*

Part Two

Summer at Beechwood Acres

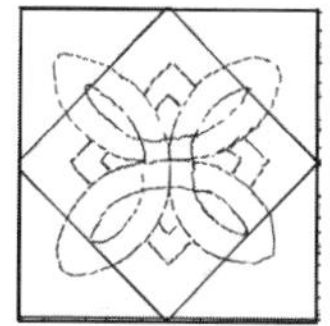

June 23

Great-Grandmother Gertrude has kept her word—the journal has arrived! It's a good thing that tomorrow is our "no-church Sunday," and we'll have a chance to read it. I've already skimmed through it and learned a lot. I could hardly put it down! My great-great-great-great-(I have no idea how many greats) grandmother, Feronica Bauer, kept the journal. She was the daughter of Conrad Bauer, who came over from the old land in a big ship in the 1700s. There were 200 people on the ship when they set sail, all eager to reach the new land with its promise of freedom of religion, and plenty of fertile soil available for the clearing of virgin forests—miles and miles of it, in fact.

They had plans to carve out farms and homesteads for themselves in the wilderness, cutting roads through it, and conquering against all odds. But misfortune was their lot, for the ship had poor sailing weather and was becalmed for over ninety days in the middle of the Atlantic Ocean. Their supply of food spoiled and became maggoty, and over half their number perished and were buried at sea. The rest arrived, sad and disillusioned, at Germantown, near Philadelphia, the City of Brotherly Love, in Penn's Woods. William Penn had offered them a refuge there and the chance to live peaceably with all men.

Young Conrad Bauer was single when he arrived, and though he had lost some of his relatives on the journey, he regained courage of heart and traveled westward through Brandywine until he reached the Conestoga Valley, the most fertile and well-watered land in Penn's Woods. There, near Earltown, a town nicknamed Saeue Schwamm Stettle (Pig Swamp Town), he eventually became the owner of 100 acres of land north of the Welsh Mountains, which was fertile and productive. Conrad married a Lutheran girl and they had eight children including Feronica, who kept the journal.

The Indians were peaceable and friendly, thanks to Penn's fair treatment of them. They had a settlement near Weber's Thal and another near Graf's Mill, northwest of the Horseshoe Trail that ran through Earltown, and on through Hickorytown.

As more settlers arrived, some pushed ever further westward, on to Harris Ferry. Many of these settlers were Swiss Anabaptists, also called Mennonites, who had been persecuted and driven from Switzerland to the Palatinate along the southern Rhine River, in Germany, and after enduring hardships there, too, welcomed the opportunity to come to America.

Life was not easy for them in the new land, even though they were no longer persecuted, for there were many trials, struggles, and dangers, as told in her journal. She had a hard life since her mother died when she was just fifteen years old causing her to be a substitute mother to her seven younger brothers and sisters. She seems to have had a buoyant spirit although, taking the hardships in stride, and rising above the difficult circumstances.

I wish I could keep Feronica's journal, but Great-grandmother Gertrude wants it back, so I'll copy it into my journal as I read it. It's a rather small, thin journal, since paper was scarce at that time. A well-to-do friend of Feronica's, the daughter of an ironmaster, was able to supply her with some, but not as much as she would have liked. I'm thankful for all she wrote and that it has been preserved until now. I wish I could spend the evening reading it, but we're invited to the Mullets' for supper and I sure don't want to miss that. It's always fun to visit there. They, along with Rachel and Ben, have become some of our dearest friends since we moved here.

June 25

A fat packet of letters came from the home folks today, long letters from Mom and all the others. That reminds me, I must write to them and tell them all about Great-grandmother Gertrude's visit. They're bursting with curiosity and I can't blame them a bit. After I've recopied the old journal, I'll have to let them read it when I get the opportunity.

And now for the first entry in Feronica's journal, when she was eighteen years old. She has no year recorded and that is a pity, but we do know that it was sometime in the 1700s. She begins:

> I take my pen in hand on this 2nd day of May of my 19th year. It was my brother Hans' 15th birthday, and he and I walked to a place several miles beyond Weber's Thal this morning with our Mennonite friends, Jacob and Lisbet, to greet the new family—the Timbelmans—who just recently moved there. They have two fine-looking sons, Yockel and Cristly (both older than Hans and me), and then two pretty girls, Rebecca, who is just my age, and Fianna, who is just a year younger, and six younger brothers and sisters in stair-step sizes. I am sure that we shall all be good friends even though we don't attend the same church. Rebecca and Fianna are friendly and jolly, and we had a lot of fun making taffy, and then the boys helped to pull it into long white strands. They are friendly and good-natured, and the whole family is of a decent sort. They invited Hans and me to attend their new church at Weber's Thal sometime, and we might just do that, for it is so far to attend our church services in Brickerville, and since Mother died, Father has been lax in attending with his family.
>
> The girls' mother, Lydia Timbelman, is a plump, bustling, motherly soul, and my heart felt pained at the thought of our own mother gone from our home forever. I thought of how it would be to have her greet us at the door when we came home, smiling a welcome, and I could give back to her the burden of responsibility on my shoulders of helping to raise the motherless younger ones.
>
> On the way home we took another trail and passed through the Indian settlement just north of Weber's Thal where the friendly tribe of Conestogas live. We watched the Indian children playing, then a woman with a bright-eyed little child in a pack on her back came to talk to us. We can understand each other well enough, with what we've learned of each other's languages. They have brightly painted willow baskets decorated with feathers and beads. They live in bark wigwams, but are learning some of the white people's ways.

We traveled on the Horseshoe Trail toward Saeue Schwamm Stettle. It was such a lovely spring day to walk through the forest—everything was green once again and the canopy of leafy foliage overhead shielded us from the sun's rays. The birds were singing sweetly, and we saw a flock of wild turkeys. The grass is already lush and thick under the oak trees. We left the trail to see a patch of wildflowers, and then we startled a mother bear with two cubs, who hurried off toward the Welsh Mountains. Jacob said it was a good thing we hadn't come between her and her cubs.

It was nice to get away for a day, but when we came home, Father had gone hunting, and Tilda was ready to hand over the responsibility of the younger ones to me. She just turned twelve and is small for her age, so she was truly glad to see us.

Little Bessie, who is three and was born the same day Mother died, was crying because she didn't feel well. She is sick so often and I wish there would be a doctor close by, or one willing to travel here to see her. There is a doctor in Brandywine, but Father says it is too far, and besides, we can't afford it. He says that perhaps she will outgrow her ailment. It may have come from having her start without Mother's milk. For her first several months we hardly expected her to live; her only sustenance was cornmeal mush we cooked and thinned. We dipped a little rag in the mush, then put a corner of it into her mouth, and she learned to suckle. It was very slow and time-consuming, but Father, Hans, Tilda, and I took turns. She didn't grow much and was very fussy; but later, when she could eat from a spoon and drink from a cup, she gained weight at last. If only she could feel well now and wouldn't need to cry so much.

At the end of Feronica's first journal entry, she had written: "O Mother, if you could only be here with us again, our house would be a place of happiness and laughter again." Then she added a Bible verse: "I will lift up mine eyes unto the hills, from whence cometh my help. My help cometh from the Lord, which made heaven and earth" (Psalm 121:1,2).

It's plain to see that life wasn't easy in those days and that Feronica had a heavy responsibility on her shoulders. She missed her mother so much, and one could almost cry for her. Still, I hope she was given the help she needed and that little Bessie was soon better. I had to think of the poem:

God's Promise

God didn't promise
days without pain,
laughter without sorrow
or sun without rain.
But God did promise
strength for the day,
comfort for the tears
and a light for the way.
And for all who believe
in His kingdom above,
He answers their faith
with everlasting love.
- Author unknown

June 26

Old Brindle, the cow, is not adjusted to being milked so early. Since daylight arrives earlier now, she's never at the barn at milking time. But going to the back end of the meadow for her is a special part of my morning—with the delightful fragrances and the early morning hush over everything and the birds' sweet chorus all around me. It is a time of meditating and basking in the beauties of God's nature.

So far, all had been quiet around the range shelter so early in the morning with the three children probably still sleeping soundly. That is, until this morning when, following the creek, I came around the bend and heard voices. I quickly dropped down and peeked through the foliage.

The older boy, Chet, was saying, "I don't think the farmer will mind that we took a few baler twines. We need something to hang our clothes on when we wash them." He was tying one end of the twine to a corner of the range shelter and the other end to a shrub.

"Wasn't that big barn neat!" Billy exclaimed. "I'm glad we saw those people going away last night and we could go and

explore. I wish we could sleep in all that straw."

"Maybe we could," Diane said thoughtfully. "We could wait until after dark, then sneak into the barn's back door, and with our flashlights find our way up that little ladder."

The older boy said, "That might be all right for next fall when the weather turns cooler, but for now it's probably much nicer here in the shelter in our sleeping bags, with the birds singing in the morning."

"But up in the barn we'd hear roosters crowing," Billy said. "I saw two roosters last night."

"If only we could have gotten some eggs," Diane said. "I'd make some omelets for breakfast. But we'd better hurry and eat our cereal and get our clothes washed now, so they can dry before that boy and girl come back to hoe their field, which they probably will one of these days. Here's the Tide soap I bought."

"I sure am hungry," Billy complained. "Did you get milk at the store, Chet?"

"Sure did," came the answer. "Remember, I came back with it just before we left to explore the big barn. I put the bottle of milk into the spring, behind a big rock. I'll go and get it now. Want to come along?"

The three children left then, and as soon as they were out of sight, I hastily herded Brindle toward the barn and was out of sight before they came back. Later I wished I had stepped out and talked to the children in a friendly way and invited them to come to the house for eggs and reassured them I won't send them back to their stepfather. Next time I will.

Kermit's busy these days with the haymaking, and the clattering of the mowing machine and the wonderful fragrance of the new-mown hay wafts on the breeze. We're hoping for more of this gorgeous weather until it's all baled.

> ***Golden Gem for today:*** *Praise is the acknowledgment of that which I have sent you. Few men would send a further gift of payment until they had received the acknowledgment of a previous one. So praise, acknowledging as it does My gift and blessing, leaves the way open for Me to shower yet more on the thankful heart.*

July 1 (Sunday)

We attended church services at the Hershbergers. In two weeks, it's our turn! It will probably be the very first time that church services were ever held on this farm. I hope we can get everything spruced up well enough. I'm making some progress on Feronica's journal. Her next entry was again about a visit to the Timbelman Homestead with their Mennonite friends, Jacob and Lisbet, this time to a stump-removing and stone-picking party. I suppose she didn't have much else to write about besides the daily grind of scrubbing clothes by hand, cooking over the open fireplace hearth, and caring for the family of motherless children, since they didn't have much of a social life and didn't often attend church. There were only a few close neighbors. Surrounded by forest as they were, they must have been rather isolated.

She begins:

> May 16 – Another memorable day. The springtime ground has heaved and settled, loosening the tree stumps, and so now is the time to remove them for those who are clearing extra fields. Jacob and Lisbet asked Hans and me to go along to the Timbelmans again, and this time we didn't have to walk. They each took one of their dad's work horses, and Lisbet and I rode double on a Haflinger mare.
>
> Horseshoe Trail is no longer as rutted as it was, so we had good riding and it seemed like we were there in no time at all. I just wish Father could buy Hans and me each a horse of our own and a two-wheeled cart, but we haven't prospered that much yet. The Ulrichs, a mile west of us, have been kind enough to loan us two of their work horses and a wagon when we go to church in Brickerville.
>
> It was another lovely day with a cool breeze blowing through the Conestoga Valley, stirring the leaves on the trees and swaying the ferns by the trail. Bobwhites called from the thickets, and a brightly colored ring-necked pheasant was startled from the underbrush as we passed. It flew away, up over the trees. Near Weber's Thal, a doe and her fawn bounded across the trail and ran into the woods. We met a man with a horse hitched to a cart, and Lisbet said that the Mennonite Church doesn't approve of those carts—they are too worldly. The old-fashioned way of riding horseback or walking is good enough for them.
>
> At the Timbelman's cabin, Yockel and Cristly came from the barn to greet Hans and Jacob, and Rebecca and Fianna met us at the door and gave us a glad welcome. I wish we would have a home like they do, with such jolly sisters and their kind and cheerful mother presiding over everything. They were baking hams, which filled the kitchen with a delightful aroma. A pot of beans was bubbling merrily on the hearth. On the shelf stood rows and rows of freshly baked rhubarb pies and golden loaves of bread, all to feed the hungry workers. Fianna told me that they have plans

to build a stone house with an oak floor, and windows with glass from Germantown, in the near future; then their old house might be used as a chicken house.

We helped the girls and their mother pluck the feathers from the geese. The feathers will be stuffed into bags and the ends sewn shut to make pillows. The rest of the forenoon we also helped pick stones from the fields and threw them into a stone boat drawn by two horses.

To remove the stumps, the men hitched a pair of oxen to a mallet lever. After the men had dug all around the stump with a spade and mattock, they fastened the mallet lever to the stump, and the oxen knew to give a quick jerk and pull hard, which dislodged the stump. It was hard work for man and beast, but it will make a smooth field for planting corn, pumpkins, and runner beans. Mrs. Timbelman, with the help of a few neighbor women, had set up a big table under the trees and spread a hearty feast for the hungry workers. It was a very enjoyable day for me.

As I carried out a bowl of parings to the hogs after dinner, I met Yockel Timbelman coming out of the barn. He said they are having a hymn sing in two weeks, in the evening, and that if I am able to come, he will take me home afterward. It was very kind of him to offer it, and I surely hope that Hans and I will be able to go. Yockel showed me their woodworking shop and the project his father is working on—making a two-wheeled cart to use to ride to church. His father is a very heavy-set man. (His nickname is *Foss*, which means barrel in German. Everyone calls him that and I don't know what his real name is.)

Yockel told me that his father weighs over 400 pounds and can't walk very far. He's too heavy to ride a horse, so it puts him in kind of a predicament for getting around. They are Mennonites, too, and Lisbet had told me that their people don't approve of the more worldly method of getting around by cart. I asked Yockel about this, and he said his father is not putting springs in the cart, and he thinks the brethren will allow this. Riding on springs is a lot more luxurious, they say, and not nearly as bumpy. I wouldn't know, for Ulrichs' wagons don't have springs either, and we jostle around on them over the rutted roads.

Yockel showed me the wood his father is using for the cart. The seats will be made of pine, and the

> spokes and shafts of ash; the rest will be of hickory. I can hardly believe that he took the time to explain and show it to little me! He is a very fine young man. Now I'm counting the days until the hymn sing! Lisbet and Jacob are planning to go, but we'll all have to walk then, for their parents are using the horses to go to Hickorytown that weekend. But I don't mind—as long as I can go—for even the walking part is like an adventure. Going away is so rare and special. If only Tilda were a little older, but I guess she'll just have to learn to take a bit more responsibility. Tonight when we came home, she had already put Bessie to sleep in her trundle bed, and there were still traces of tears on her cheeks from her continual crying. Father; Mart, age ten; and David, who is eight, were busy at building a stake and rider fence. The two little boys, Joey, six, and Jeems, five, were playing with their puppy.

At the end of her journal entry, Feronica had drawn a circlet of flowers around a Bible verse: "This is the day which the Lord hath made; we will rejoice and be glad in it" (Psalm 118:24).

Ya well, it is time for me to go; Kermit and Jared have finished the chores and we plan to play a game of croquet. But, I think I'll take the time to copy an inspirational thought first.

> **Golden Gem for today:** *Let the Sabbath calm enwrap your minds and hearts. Let it be a rest from the worry and fret of life, a halt by the busy highway when you seek some rest and shade.*

July 2

Today the temperature was ninety degrees in the shade. Towards chore time, the sky darkened and we began to hear ominous rumbles of thunder in the west, and jagged lightning flashed from cloud to cloud. We decided to wait to eat supper until after the chores were done, for there was a kind of heavy stillness in the air and the sky had a greenish hue. A car came tearing in the drive and stopped, the gravel flying. It was Mirabelle Oleson, and she came to tell us that there were tornado warnings and we should be prepared to run to the cellar if necessary. The

storm was due to arrive within a half-hour, so we hurried to the barn to care for the stock as well as we could.

The wind whipped around the corners of the barn as lightning flashed. Jared and Treva were herding the cows into the barn when we heard a yell. Fearing that something was wrong, Kermit and I hurried to the doorway. Jared was pointing toward the meadow. We saw three figures, running hand-in-hand, yelling and crying. It was the campers, running for shelter from the storm. Big drops of rain were beginning to splash down, and the wind was picking up force. But when the oldest boy, Chet, saw us standing at the barn door, he suddenly stopped in his tracks, trying to pull the others back. Billy was sobbing. Diane, looking over her shoulder at the menacing stormy sky, tried to pull Chet toward the barn.

"Hurry," she gasped. "We'll be caught in the storm!"

"Yes, come on in," Kermit urged them. "Don't be frightened." So the three children came hand-in-hand to the door, a look of relief on their faces.

"Let's all head for the house," Kermit said. "We'll go through the south barn door—it's closer."

In a few minutes we were in the kitchen. I lit the gas lantern because the sky had become even darker and had opened up, dumping torrents of water. Kermit went to the west window, scanning the skies, so that he could tell us when to head for the cellar. But everything was so dark and the wind was lashing the tree branches, so Kermit decided it would be best to go immediately.

Just after we got to the cellar, we heard a roaring sound overhead. Suddenly, all was quiet. But it was only a lull in the storm—soon it was back. The children huddled together with their arms around each other. Billy was still sobbing, Diane was shivering, and Chet was doing his best to comfort and reassure them.

Although it seemed to last a long time, the worst of the storm was soon over, and we headed back up to the kitchen. The temperature had quickly dropped, and I started a fire in the cook stove. It was raining outside so we couldn't go out to check for storm damage right away. The children sat politely on the settee, and we pulled up chairs near them to hear more of their story. At first they wouldn't say much, but when Kermit reassured them we wouldn't tell their stepfather they were here, they began to talk.

Billy had dried his tears and got a big smile on his face when Treva passed a plate of cookies. "We ran away from Pop," he said, "and we never want to go back."

"Hush!" Diane scolded. "We might go back sometime."

Chet spoke up then, "We'll probably go back this fall when school starts. We like camping out, and we'll be fine."

"What school did you go to?" Treva wondered. "Didn't they even miss you?"

Diane shook her head. "Duffy home schools us, and we were just finished with the term when she broke her leg. I suppose

Pop thought she took us with her to her sister's. Our mother lives in Texas."

Poor, poor children. We gave them soft beds to sleep in tonight. We'll decide what to do another time.

July 3

This morning the three campers joined our household for a hearty breakfast of scrapple, eggs, and oatmeal, which seemed to revive their spirits. After the chores were done, they were soon ready to head out to their range shelter and continue camping. Treva packed them a picnic lunch; and we told them to come to the house for fresh eggs and milk every morning. Jared loaned Chet his slingshot.

When Billy asked Kermit if they could sleep in the barn sometime, Kermit gave his permission as long as they took no matches with them. They stayed to watch as we did the chores. Billy made friends with the cocker spaniel pup, and Diane especially loved the horses. They all watched me milk the cow and then headed for the meadow, waving until they were out of sight among the trees.

There had been very little storm damage to the farm, although two of our oldest apple trees in the orchard were down. This wasn't really a loss to us because the trees were too old to bear fruit anyway. A corner of the barn roof had a few shingles missing, but it didn't take Kermit long to fix that.

Now we'll have to decide what to do about the three children. Who could we ask advice without causing the children any more hardships? We'll have to talk it over.

> ***Golden Gem for today:*** *Never judge. The heart of man is so delicate, so complex, only its Maker can know it. Each heart is so different, actuated by different motives, controlled by different circumstances, and influenced by different sufferings.*

July 8 (Sunday)

We'll have a busy week ahead getting ready for church services here a week from today. Treva and Jared persuaded us to go on a picnic today, and we invited the three campers to go along.

We chose a spot down near the island, and we spread our tablecloth there under the trees. The children have lost their shyness around us and played happily, wading and splashing in the water and playing a game of tag. When it was time for us to go back home, they stood looking after us (a bit wistfully, I thought) and waving until we were out of sight. What, oh what, should we do about them?

Now for some more of Feronica's journal. It is so interesting to read about what the Conestoga Valley was like in the 1700s. She writes:

> May 22 – We took another long walk today to see The Settlement of the Solitary [later called Ephrata Cloister]. Hans had to make a trip to Eby's Mill, so it was just Jacob, Lisbet, and I. (I'm afraid if it weren't for them, I'd have a very dull life, with all work and no play.)
>
> We started early in the morning, when the birds were just awakening and rabbits were hopping about, looking for clover. The grass under the trees was like a thick green carpet where we took a shortcut through the woods. We crossed the Conestoga Creek on a swinging footbridge and sat for awhile watching the water gurgling over the rocks as it flowed westward toward the mighty Susquehanna. As we sat there, the green fern fronds on the bank parted and a wild turkey gobbler came to the water to drink, followed by a hen and her poults. Just then a movement on the other bank caught my eye, and there stood a graceful buck, its eyes alert to any surrounding dangers. He took a drink and then disappeared into the woods.
>
> As we approached The Settlement of the Solitary, Lisbet told me all she knew about the place. The leader and founder is Conrad Beissel who claims to have had special visions and revelations from God, and he believes that a spiritual person does not marry. He is a minister of the First German Baptist congregation and has quite a group of followers. According to Lisbet, even some of the Mennonites are convinced that his is the true way to holiness. Throughout the Conestoga Valley and beyond, his followers have left their homes and moved into his settlement. Forbidding marriage,

he has even encouraged some wives to leave their husbands, and husbands to leave their wives, in order to move into his settlement. Lisbet said that one man was so afraid his wife would desert him and move to the Settlement, that he tied her to the bedpost!

When we approached the place, we saw a big gray building with hand-split clapboards, and dormer windows in every story. Cloistered all around it were more buildings and little cabins. We learned that one building is called The Sister House, and one is called The Brother House. Another is called The House of Prayer, and there are also a lot of little cabins where people live in solitude.

The people there think it is wrong to eat meat and they keep Saturday as the Sabbath day and work on Sunday. They do a lot of good, too, by baking bread to give to the poor. Some of the sisters do weaving and drawing of religious texts, decorating them with intricate designs.

Lisbet said they lead austere lives, sleeping on hard, narrow, wooden benches with a block of wood for a pillow. Some do so much fasting that they are malnourished. Meals are meager, and it is said that one woman there lives entirely on acorn bread and nothing else.

There is a bakery and a printing shop. They make their own paper and bind their books with leather tanned in the Settlement. A kind lady showed us around the place. Conrad Beissel wasn't there, and I was sorry, because I would have liked to meet him. Lisbet and Jacob said it's a good thing he wasn't there—he might have tried to persuade us to join them. The doorways are low, to teach people humility by stooping low when they go through them.

When we left, Lisbet declared emphatically that she wishes to always stay a Mennonite and to eat plenty of meat so that she stays hale and hearty for the rigors of frontier life. Jacob teased her mercilessly, saying that she would marry a hale and hearty Dutchman and have at least a dozen hale and hearty children. She tried to box his ears, and he leapt aside and tripped over a root, startling a rabbit out of the thickets.

On the way home we took another route. Jacob wanted to show us Hans Graf's place. He must be one of the most prosperous men in the area, because he has a beautiful stone house and big barns. Jacob said that when Hans Graf's oldest son and their hired man

> were looking for their runaway horses, they came to a place where there were large, beautiful oak trees in a lush meadow where three bubbling springs flowed out of the ground and made a stream of water. They figured that the soil there must be the most fertile in the area, and that the springs would never dry up, so they built their homestead there. It's a beautiful place. We took a drink of the spring water—the sweetest and purest I ever tasted. It surely refreshed us for the rest of the walk home.
>
> The day had turned warm, and we were glad for the coolness and shade of the woods. Lisbet told me the story of Hans Graf's two marriages, but that will have to wait until next time. It's time to get the bath water ready for the boys and to tell Bessie her good-night story.

Feronica again ended her day's entry in the journal with a Bible verse encircled with a border of flowers. It was: "For the commandment is a lamp; and the law is light; and reproofs of instruction are the way of life" (Proverbs 6:23).

She must have had an interest in spiritual things even though they didn't often attend church, because she must have read her Bible. *Ya well,* Kermit will soon be in from checking on the stock, and we want to go to bed early in order to be rested for our busy week ahead.

An inspirational verse:

> ***Golden Gem for today:*** *Turn out from your hearts and lives all that is not loving, so shall ye bear fruit, and by this all men shall know ye are My disciples because ye have love toward one another.*

July 15 (Sunday)

The sun is setting in a maze of splendid colors tonight as Kermit and I sit on the front porch. He is scanning the *Budget*, and I'm writing in my diary. Treva, Jared, Chet, Diane, and Billy, are playing croquet on the front lawn. The children are spending more and more time here with us; and if we hadn't been so busy getting ready for church services here, we might already have done something about the situation.

It is hard to believe that this long-planned-for day is nearly over, but it's a good feeling, too. The Mullets' oldest daughter came to help us get ready and stayed from Thursday until Saturday evening. She has all kinds of energy, and with her help, we got everything shipshape around here. Kermit, Treva, and Jared were busy in the fields, so we were able to have some sisterly chats, as we worked together much of the time.

As we were working out in the yard on Friday, and our three little campers had come to play with our cocker pup, Mirabelle Oleson unexpectedly dropped in. When she heard the story of the children, she was aghast! She said we could get into serious trouble by not reporting them at once to the authorities. I told her we promised the children we wouldn't tell their stepfather where they are, but she cast that idea aside as if it was not important. She said that things would be checked out by the authorities, and if their stepfather is abusive, they would be put into a foster home.

Since we were so busy getting ready for church, we decided to put it off until Monday. I hope it wasn't wrong of us to do so.

We had a nice amount of visitors here at church today, but no visiting ministers, so our usual preacher had the main sermon. It was truly inspiring as the harmonious singing filled the rooms and echoed back from the ceiling. I felt so thankful for the privilege of religious freedom for which our ancestors crossed the ocean. The simple meal afterwards was adequate for the situation, and we even had *snitz boi*, thanks to Rachel who had come over on Saturday to help make them.

> ***Verse for today:*** *"Where two or three are gathered together in My name, there am I in the midst of them" (Matthew 18:20).*

July 17

This morning Treva got stung by an angry, buzzing bee. The sole of her foot swelled to almost twice its size. She wasn't able to help in the fields, so at Diane's insistence, she paid the range shelter a visit. Chet and Diane pulled her there on the wagon, not minding all the bumps and jolts, and treated her like a guest of honor. They built a campfire and roasted doggies for their lunch—this time they had ketchup. It was wash day for them, and the wash line had been strung up again from the shelter to a shrub. Tee shirts and overalls flapped in the breeze.

An old stump was their makeshift table, and Chet brought water from the spring to fill the mugs. In the afternoon they played games, and then entertained Treva by performing a little skit for her.

When Treva was not back by suppertime, Kermit and I walked down to visit our young friends, too. We knew that it was high time to do something about them. When we got near, we heard the happy chattering and laughter of the children. They had a campfire going and were cooking something in a frying pan. The delicious aroma of frying fish drifted over to us, and we almost felt like traitors coming to spoil their happiness.

Billy called, "Hurrah! More visitors! You can sit right here on this log and I'll get you each a fish sandwich."

We joined their little feast of happiness, sharing it with them for awhile, then mustered courage and began our serious talk. We explained to them what Mirabelle Oleson had said and that something must be done. Billy began to cry, rubbing his eyes with his fists, and Chet looked troubled and unhappy.

Diane's face was woebegone, too, but then her face suddenly lit up. "I know!" she cried happily. "You could call our Aunt Jean. She's very nice, but she lives in Georgia. Maybe she would come and get us." So that is what we did. Diane knew her aunt's name and town, and we were able to find the number through directory assistance.

With very good timing, Mirabelle Oleson had dropped in soon after we all arrived back at the house, and she took us to her house to use the phone. Diane talked to her aunt, then I talked to her, too. She seemed like a nice lady and was very concerned about the children. She wondered if we could keep them at our house until she came for them, and then she would decide what she would do about the situation.

It is a load off our minds to have it taken care of, and Mirabelle feels better about it too. Now we have three young boarders at our house for awhile. I think there will never be a dull moment!

A day of working from dawn to dusk, and now it's time to rest. Our first batch of sweet corn is ready for market (and for eating fresh at mealtime!). Our three little boarders just love it. I don't believe they ever had fresh sweet corn right out of the garden. They're all out in the field getting a ride on the big flat wagon pulled by the two large work horses.

While I rest my tired feet, I'll copy some more of Feronica's journal. She writes:

> May 31 – Last evening was the hymn sing at the Timbelman's, and it was an exciting evening. Rebecca and Fianna had invited their friends from miles around, and we all enjoyed it so much that we decided to have it again in four weeks.
>
> The large barn on their property had plenty of room for all the young folks, both for the singing and for the party games afterwards. They plan to have gatherings there every two to four weeks. It was rather late by the time we sang the parting hymn (the singing was truly beautiful), so Rebecca and Fianna persuaded Lisbet, Jacob, Hans, and me to stay for the night; then we could walk home today. We were the only ones who hadn't come on horseback, except for the closest neighbors. The boys slept in the hay mow in the barn, and the girls slept on straw ticks on the loft floor.
>
> In a way I was disappointed that Yockel did not get the chance to take me home after all, but we were able to have a few words together while playing Blind Man's Bluff. All he said was, "In two weeks," but I knew what he meant, for he winked at the same time.
>
> One of Hans Graf's sons was there, too, and that reminds me, I haven't written the story of how his father came to have two wives. It wasn't intentional; everyone felt very sorry for him and just as sorry for both his wives.
>
> When Hans still lived in Switzerland, his father was a rich and well-known government official. Hans followed in his father's footsteps, and after he had gone through training to be a general in the army, he married a girl who was also of high rank. They had one son, then much to his wife's dismay, Hans became influenced by Anabaptist teachings. He was re-bap-

> tized, choosing to suffer persecution with the people of God, turning his back on his riches and position. His wife did not share his beliefs. She refused to leave the state church, so Hans left Switzerland without her.
>
> He still loved his wife and returned to Switzerland a number of times to beg her to join him in America. This was done in utmost secrecy, because the law forbade her to help him in any way or she would be cast into prison. When their son was five years old, Hans had him brought to America. Soon after that, some immigrants told Hans that his wife had died.
>
> Hans later married a second time to a young woman named Anna Herr, and they moved to Strasburg. They had been married for over twenty years and had nine children when Hans' brother, Martin Graf, came to America. He informed Hans that his first wife was still living—it was someone else by the same name who had died. What a shock that must have been!
>
> Hans could not rightfully live with his second wife anymore. Soon after, his first wife became an Anabaptist and came to America to find her husband and son. It was unbelievable to her to find that her husband had another family in America, but she took the blame upon herself. Hans built a cabin for her and a small one for himself, choosing to live in solitude the rest of his life. He provided for his two wives and their families, and the three of them lived peaceably, in righteousness, making the best of the situation. Someone said of Hans, "He is a respected, faithful witness wherever he goes."

That is quite a story about how they were faithful to the end. Kermit said that nowadays people divorce and remarry at will, thinking that there is nothing wrong with it. And yet, God's laws never change, be it in the eighteenth century or in the twenty-first.

Our three boarders and our *Maad* and *Gnecht* are merrily trooping into the house now, so I'll lay this aside and set out a snack of milk and cookies for them. This morning Billy said he hopes they can stay here forever and ever. (Smiles.)

July 20

The children's aunt called from Georgia this morning and asked if we could keep the children until she gets things settled with their stepfather. It rained heavily all day, and it was good to know that the children were safe. If the creek should rise, that range shelter might be carried away downstream.

Kermit and Jared spent the day helping a neighbor put stabling into his barn, and Treva went along to help Mom Mullet for the day. I got some sewing done, and now I'll copy more of Feronica's journal. Her next entry was June 18. She wrote:

> Hans and I attended Mennonite church services at Weber's Thal on Sunday with Jacob and Lisbet. We arrived early, and I saw *Foss* Timbelman drive in on his new horse-drawn cart, the one Yockel had shown me. Yockel and Cristly were there, too, riding in on horseback at the same time we arrived. Yockel sure is good-looking! They stopped to talk to us for a few minutes, and it was then that a movement on the other side of the road caught our eye.
>
> Someone had stepped out of the trees, then quickly ran back into the woods again. Something white in the crook of a low tree branch gleamed in the early morning sunlight, and Yockel and Cristly went to see what it was. It was a pack of pamphlets put there by one of Conrad Beissel's followers, proclaiming that Saturday should be kept as the Sabbath day and divine services should be held then as their congregation does. I guess the Settlement of the Solitary will not be satisfied until they have converted more Mennonites.
>
> Cristly threw the pamphlets in the gutter and scuffed dirt over them. We then filed into the church which is made of wood and has new wooden benches. The boys and men sit on one side of the room, and the women and girls sit on the other side. In the center there is a table where the song leaders sit, and the minister stands at one end to preach. I'm glad that I know German as well as English, and that I could understand the sermon.
>
> The preacher was very solemn, warning against false teachings and religions. The brethren were exhorted to remain true to the faith. He preached against worldliness, and I thought I saw him look intently at Yockel's father, *Foss* Timbelman, the only one who had come to church on a horse-drawn cart.

The brethren disapproved of these carts, even though there were no springs. The congregation sang a few German songs both before and after the message, and then when we were dismissed, we filed outside.

Most everyone stayed awhile to visit, and as we stood around talking, a sad thing happened. A young girl, not much older than I, who had come on horseback, led her horse to the big mounting stone, and climbed on her horse's back. The horse was skittish and high strung. He suddenly began to rear and buck, throwing the girl off. She landed on the rock and lay white and still. She was still unconscious when the men hastily made a litter and placed her on it to carry her home, followed by her weeping mother. We were all very subdued as we walked home, not knowing whether or not the girl would recover.

On the way home, we met more travelers on the Horseshoe Trail as we were going toward Saeue Schwamm Stettle. They had walked all the way from Hickorytown and were on their way to Germantown.

After supper, Father put on his best clothes and went on a mysterious visit. Oh dear, are we going to have a stepmother soon? In a way it would be a relief to share the cares and responsibilities of mothering a family with someone older, at least if she were someone nice like the Widow Magdalena.

Hans wanted to go fishing in the evening, but I knew Father wouldn't have allowed it on a Sunday, so we all went for a walk along the creek. Hans carried Bessie most of the way, for I don't think she ever really feels well. If only we could have a doctor for her. She enjoyed seeing the creek though, and hearing the water gurgling over the rocks. She played on the grassy bank selecting the nicest stones out of the shallow water for her collection. The boys tried their hands at skipping stones over the water at the deeper parts. I sat on the bank, dangling my feet in the water—glad for the peace and solitude and the time to sort out my tangled thoughts.

What if Yockel asks me for a date and wants me to join the Mennonites? Would I say yes? But maybe it's all just a notion of mine and he has no such intentions at all.

Another flower-bordered Bible verse concluded Feronica's entry: "Come unto Me all ye that labour and are heavy laden, and

I will give you rest. Take my yoke upon you and learn of me; for I am meek and lowly in heart, and ye shall find rest unto your souls" (Matthew 11:28,29).

Ya well, it's time to start the chores. Kermit and the children will soon be home for supper. I've been sitting here thinking about Feronica while I watch the rain streaming down against the windowpanes. I wonder, will she join the Mennonites and marry Yockel? Then I had to laugh at myself, for those early settlers in the Conestoga Valley are long dead and buried, and the joys, tears, and heartaches of that time are long gone.

> ***Golden Gem for today:*** *Be watchful to hear My voice and instantly to obey. Obedience is your great sign of faith. "Why call ye me Lord, Lord, and do not the things that I say" was My word when on earth to the many who followed and heard, but did not do.*

July 25

The children are helping to pick produce and to pack it for market. Chet and Diane are surprisingly good helpers, and Billy keeps us all entertained with his antics and his endless questions. His favorite thing to do is to sneak around the house and the shrubbery with his slingshot, looking for hapless sparrows to zap. That suits us fine, because we have to keep their numbers down or else our precious martin birds will move away. Billy also spends a lot of time playing with our cocker pup. Sometimes they sit out on the road bank and wave to passers-by.

Both Billy and Chet are very interested in the guinea pigs that Jared is raising. He is hoping to make a bit of profit out of it, but prices are down so he told the boys they can have the guinea pigs. The boys see to it that the animals have fresh grass to eat every day and plenty of clean water. Tonight I took a walk out to the orchard and discovered that the youngsters had built a tree house in one of the apple trees. It seems they are enjoying themselves here and having wholesome fun.

Treva helped Diane make a playhouse in the old shed, making toy appliances out of empty cardboard boxes and draping them with the fabric Mirabelle had given them. After it was all finished, they invited Mirabelle and me in for tea. They served cookies and tea with style and flourish on the old china tea set that Grandma Annie had given me years ago.

Yesterday, Kermit brought home a bag of crushed ice from town, and we made a freezer full of homemade raspberry ice cream. Each of the children wanted to take a turn cranking until it got too hard for them, then it was ready to eat. Just as we were ready to scoop out servings of ice cream, Mr. Bradford dropped in, and I wondered how he had timed it so well. Later, Kermit told me that he had stopped in at Mr. Bradford's place on the way home from town and invited him over. He is a very interesting old man; he knows a lot of things that happened to the old-timers of this area in the bygone days. I suppose there aren't too many of his friends living anymore. He even entertained the children by singing a little song to them that he learned in his school days, and they loved it. Treva says he's quite a character.

Oh, yes, I nearly forgot to write the news that Emily Simmons sent in today's mail. She has a new baby brother named Ethan! I find myself wishing that I'd still be living there so I would get the chance to baby-sit him. I guess I'll have to wait until we visit them sometime to hold and cuddle him.

August 3

More of Feronica's journal. Her next entry is dated July 2. She writes:

> Hans and I attended the hymn sing at Timbelman's on Saturday evening, and, true to his word, Yockel escorted me home afterwards. We had all gone on horseback this time (using Jacob and Lisbet's horses).
>
> Yockel and I started for home as soon as the last song was sung. He was on his big, black stallion. He had sad news to tell. The girl who was thrown from her horse two weeks ago had died soon afterward. Oh, how her parents and brothers and sisters must be grieving at the loss of their loved one, who was snatched away while in the bloom of youth and health. But God's ways are not our ways, and if she had given

her heart to the Lord and was ready, she is now in a far better place.

We stopped under the trees to talk, near the banks of the Conestoga Creek. It was a beautiful spot, with the moonlight streaming down through the foliage above. Yockel is so kind and sincere, and I think I could love him, if that is what he has in mind. He wants to find land on which to build a homestead someday, maybe a little farther west.

Last night holds a dear place in my memory—it was a beautiful evening, with the night insects calling, the fireflies flickering among the trees, and the water murmuring over the rocks as it flowed on its way westward. It felt so peaceful and right being there with Yockel and I was almost sorry when it was time to head for home, yet I want to search my heart further before I make any commitment.

Father has indeed been going to see Widow Magdalena—he arrived home about the same time we did and spoke a few words to Yockel before he left. Afterwards Father and I sat on the stoop and talked. He approves of Yockel and thinks the Mennonites are fine folks and will give his blessing if I want to join. He and Magdalena plan to marry in November, so that will mean a big change for our household—surely one for the better. Magdalena has been a widow for over two years and is the mother of two small children. She is well thought of by all.

Another Bible verse and flowers concluded her entry: "Seek ye first the kingdom of God, and his righteousness; and all these things shall be added unto you" (Matthew 6:33).

August 15

Chet, Diane, and Billy are no longer here; their aunt has worked things out to take them to live with her, and they departed happily. Billy wanted to know if they could come back next summer, but I had to tell him that we might not be living here anymore. They'll probably never forget their experiences on the island, living in the old range shelter, cooking over a campfire, and washing their clothes in the creek. Maybe someday we'll get to see them again.

It seems as if the summer has simply flown—it's hard to believe that in three weeks school will be starting again. We've worked things out to have Treva and Jared attend school here. They've made a lot of friends in this district, and both say they're glad for the chance to stay awhile longer. There will be plenty of fall work to do yet before the first frost comes, so we'll be glad for their help.

Golden Gem for today: *You are building up an unshakable faith. Be furnishing the quiet places of your soul now. Fill them with all that is harmonious and good, beautiful and enduring.*

August 16

The watermelon crop is a good one this year, and we've been busy loading them for market. They sure must like that sandy soil down by the creek, for they're huge and sweet. What is more refreshing than a piece of cold watermelon on a summer day?

While I sit here on the back porch enjoying the beauty of the evening, I'll copy some more of Feronica's journal. Her next entry is dated September 3. She writes:

> I have been busy whitewashing these last few days, for we want to make everything as presentable as possible before Father's new wife, Magdalena, arrives. Hans started a fire outside under the big furnace kettle filled with water and shoveled scoops of hot coals into the boiling water and lime. It sizzled and steamed until it thickened into a paste that seemed right for brushing. I stirred it with the big wooden stirrer, then when it became too thick, Hans added more water. Finally, it was just the right thickness, and he scooped out bucketsful to cool. I whitewashed the cabin and the woodshed, and even the tree trunks closest to the buildings. I like whitewashing—it makes things look bright and new, but it doesn't stay that way very long. My dress and apron were accidentally smeared with the white lime mixture—I even had a dab on my nose—when I heard the jangling of a bell and a jolly voice singing:
>
> *Here comes Ebenezer the peddler man,*
> *Come out to my wagon and buy all you can*
> *Of pots and pans and sugar and spice,*
> *Dress goods and thread, and all that's nice.*
>
> An old swaybacked horse hitched to a rattling old wagon came into view, and sure enough, it was old Ebenezer. I'd been waiting for him for days, because Father said when the peddler comes, we could buy yard goods for new dresses for the wedding, something

that's finer than calico. I chose a piece of wine-colored chintz, Tilda chose indigo blue, and we all got buttons and thread, a packet of needles, white home-spun linen for shirts for the boys, and material for new breeches.

Now we're looking for the shoemaker to come into this area one of these days, too, to make new shoes for us. Hans says he wants buckles on his shoes, and I'd love to have ivory buttons on mine. This would be a very happy and exciting time if it weren't for Bessie's illness. She seems to be wasting away, and I must speak to Father again about sending for a doctor. I believe he thinks it's all right to wait until he has a wife to look after us all, but I think it should be now. Bessie cries so pitifully when she's not feeling well.

For her Bible verse for that day's entry, Feronica had copied, "Cast thy burden upon the Lord, and He shall sustain thee" (Psalm 55:22a). Also, "Casting all your care upon Him; for He careth for you" (I Peter 5:7).

My heart goes out to her even now, for her concerns about her little sister and without a mother to share things with and lean on. I suppose there was no such thing as a hospital in those days, in that area anyway, and they had no idea what ailed the child, since there was no doctor nearby to make a diagnosis. Life surely wasn't easy in those days, but they were stalwart and sturdy people—they had to be. I suppose it was survival of the fittest.

August 27

Signs of the approaching autumn can be seen here and there—oh, where has the summer flown to? Silo-filling time is approaching, and Pop Mullet and his boys are planning to help Kermit here at Beechwood Acres Farm. Harvesting the fields should be a breeze with their experienced help.

We're thinking of planning a trip back east to my parents sometime; it seems so long since we've seen them. Then we'll also hunt up Pamela Styer and see about that wedding gift she promised us. We know she won't be satisfied without giving us a lot!

I picked three bushels of lima beans this morning, and Kermit's going to help me hull them. Rachel and Ben are coming over, too. That will be fun!

> ***Golden Gem for today:*** *Though thou fallest often—yea many times a day, yet as many times rise again, and thou wilt find Me nigh. Thou shalt know that He which hath begun a good work in thee will perform it until the end. Though thou fallest, yet shall thou not be cast away, for I will uphold thee with Mine hand.*

September 1

More of Feronica's journal, which is dated October 6:

> Autumn is coming. The sumac in the fence row is aflame with brightness, and soon the leaves on the trees will be changing color. Then the golden leaves will fall, floating down on the breeze all around our cabin, as they do every year. This year they will also be falling on little Bessie's grave. Our hearts are heavy as we lift our eyes to the little graveyard on the hill. Our little Bessie lies beneath the sod, yet we rejoice that her spirit is free and she needs to suffer no more. She was so frail and weak at the end that we felt it was a blessing when she could go to be with the angels. But, oh, how we miss her.
>
> It was just two weeks ago today (it seems much longer) that Father finally was able to get a doctor out from Brandywine. What a relief it was to see him coming through the woods on horseback, holding on to his satchel with one hand. But what a terrible disappointment it was to find that the doctor was a bit tipsy—he must have stopped at a tavern and indulged. His speech was slurred, and I did not trust him at all. He insisted that Bessie needed a blood-letting to reduce her fever and ordered Father to get a basin.
>
> There was nothing I could do, so I went outside under the big oak tree beside the barn and covered my ears; tears were streaming down my face. It did not make sense to take away Bessie's life-giving blood—the child was already weak and frail.
>
> When the doctor emerged from the cabin, he was in high spirits and said that by morning Bessie would

be fine. He sang loudly as he mounted his horse and rode off towards Saeue Schwamm Stettle.

I tiptoed back to Bessie's side where she lay in her little trundle bed, and, indeed, she seemed better—so relaxed and calm. Her breathing was quieter, too, and hope flared in my heart that maybe she would have a good night's sleep and be all right in the morning. But at midnight Father woke me and said that Bessie had fallen asleep—the sleep that knows no awakening on this earth. I went outside and flung myself down on the grass under the oak tree and cried until I felt drained and lifeless.

Hans was sent to tell the neighbors, and as the sun started to rise in the east, neighbors began to arrive. Lisbet, Jacob, and their parents came. Father sent for Magdalena so she could sew a shroud. Lisbet's father made a small pine coffin. Burial was the next day, and I was surprised to see Yockel there. The sympathy in his eyes gave me courage as I followed the rest of the family to the little graveyard. A neighbor man said a prayer over the grave, then we sadly returned to the house. I wanted to speak to Yockel, but he was gone before I had a chance. It cheered me that he cared enough to come.

The house seems empty now with Bessie gone, but we would not wish her back to this vale of tears. Father bids us to be of good courage, and we have something to look forward to—when Magdalena comes in November. Surely she will bring warmth, love, and cheer to our household.

Feronica's Bible verse for the day was: "In the world ye shall have tribulation, but be of good cheer, I have overcome the world" (John 16:33b).

September 4

Today is the first day of school, and since Treva and Jared have quite a distance to go, Pop Mullet sent their pony and cart for them to use to drive to school. I even felt a bit envious of them this morning, as I remembered my school days. I have a bad head cold and can't talk loud, so I'll content myself with journal writing.

Feronica's next entry was about the fall harvest, written in early November when they were preparing for their father's upcoming wedding. She wrote:

> Things are going better at last, for whenever I think of Bessie, I can see her with Mother in the happy Gloryland, and my sad feelings fly away.
>
> Last week we had a happy day. My friend Lisbet and I walked to Timbelman's to Rebecca and Fianna's comfort-knotting. They had invited a group of girls, so it was very enjoyable to be there.
>
> The walk was lovely, for we were having Indian summer weather. Some of the leaves were still on the trees, and crimson vines still trailed here and there. The dry leaves crunched under our feet, and pheasants and wild turkeys called from the thickets. We visited the Indian settlement north of Weber's Thal and watched the women making hominy. They are very friendly, and even though some of them don't speak our language, their eyes and smiles were friendly.
>
> Two women were shoveling hot embers into a big pot to make lye. It sizzled and steamed, then they poured in the shelled corn. Another woman stirred the mixture with a long, thin tree branch, as clouds of steam arose to the treetops. Eventually the hulls floated to the top and the hominy was soon ready to grind. A young Indian girl, just about our own age, showed us how the hominy was ground into grits with a mortar and pestle. Nearby, the delicious aroma of roasting corn filled the air and made us hungry.
>
> The Indian girl went into a wigwam and came out with two strands of indigo blue beads—one for each of us. We accepted the gifts and thanked her and soon went on our way. But I guess I can't wear those beads if I become a Mennonite. Oh, well, I can give them to Tilda.
>
> Lisbet and I finally arrived at the Timbelman home. There we joined the other girls for several hours of comfort-knotting.
>
> After the comforter had been knotted and bound and the girls began to start for home, Fianna beckoned me to the wash house. Yockel surprised me by stepping out from behind the door. We went for a short walk through the woods back of their house, and it was good to know that he still cares for me, even though I

haven't fully made up my mind yet. I guess the trouble is that I'm still too young and don't want to think of getting married at all. There are so many cares and responsibilities in raising a family.

Our harvesting is finished now; the storeroom is filled with sacks of dried apples, pears, grapes, and tea. Strings of onions and bags of dried string beans hang from the rafters, and bushels of walnuts are laid on the loft floor to dry. In the root cellar are piles and piles of turnips, beets, pumpkins, squash, cabbages, and apples covered with hay to keep them dry.

Lisbet's mother helped us make apple butter, and we carried at least a dozen crocks of it to the loft, covered with waxed brown paper to keep it from spoiling.

This week we've finished with the hog butchering, and pork is a welcome respite from venison. Now we

> have a good supply of cured bacon and hams hanging in the smokehouse, too—Father knows how to use just the right amount of hickory wood on the smoldering fire to give it a good taste and to preserve them. The crocks of puddin's and scrapple are enough to last us for the winter.
>
> Magdalena came for half a day and helped me to make soap; now our winter supply of blocks of soap are stored in the loft. We have had a bountiful year and are richly blessed with plenty of provisions. Our hard work has paid off, and now we can enjoy the fruits of our labors when the snow flies and the wind howls around the corners of our cabin.
>
> The year I was twelve, we had such a dry year and our provisions were so scanty that had it not been for our Indian friends, we might have starved. I'm so thankful that our larder is bountiful this year, for in a few weeks our stepmother will be coming. I have a lot of sewing to do before the wedding, so I'd better get busy.

Feronica's flower-bordered Bible verse was: "In every thing give thanks: for this is the will of God in Christ Jesus concerning you" (I Thessalonians 5:18).

September 21

Mrs. Elegant, the owner of this farm, stopped in tonight to tell us that Beechwood Acres Farm will be sold in November! That means that unless the person who buys it lets us continue to rent it, we will have to find another place to move, come spring. We had been hoping that she would wait another year to sell it.

Wouldn't it be nice if Pop Mullet could buy it and let us farm it for a few more years! As it is, we'll just have to see what happens. I surely am not looking forward to moving again so soon.

Part Three

Fall at Beechwood Acres

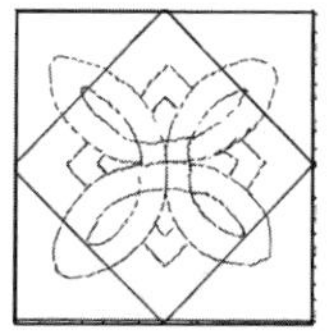

September 24

The rows of chrysanthemums along the fence are flaunting their autumn beauty, as honking wild geese wing their way overhead. We've had a killing frost, so the rest of the flowers are frozen brown. Next year someone else might be cleaning out my garden and yard and raking the leaves, and we might be living somewhere else.

Soon the wedding season will be here, and my thoughts keep turning to Feronica and her father's upcoming wedding. I wonder if they were busy with the corn husking, too, as we are, besides the sewing. Every evening after school Jared and Treva help until nearly dark, then we all come in, hungry for the mush simmering on the stove and the potatoes and meat roasting in the oven.

I'll copy more of Feronica's journal while I wait for Kermit to come in from the barn. Her next entry was November 19. She wrote:

> The wedding is planned for next week. I just finished my new wine-colored chintz dress, and I finished Tilda's blue one last week. Magdalena made the boys' breeches and new shirts and brought them over tonight; now at last I feel that we are ready. Father thinks that it's very unnecessary to make such a to-do about having new clothes, but I don't want Magdalena to think that we are shiftless. I'd rather work my fingers to the bone than have her think that. It sure is a good feeling to have the sewing done and to have so much food preserved for the winter. Hans and Father have chopped the biggest pile of firewood ever and stacked it against the side of the cabin. Father is talking of getting one of those new iron cook stoves on his next trip to Germantown and I hope he does, for it would make the cooking so much easier.

Magdalena and I were able to have a heart-to-heart talk tonight while we hemmed handkerchiefs. She told me how her first husband died—it was two years ago in the spring. She had gone with her husband to Eby's Mill with two horses hitched to the wagon. Her sister was staying with them at the time, so their little three-year-old daughter was left with her (something she has been thankful for ever since).

When they approached the Pequea Creek, they saw that the water was rising fast; a storm up-country had dumped a lot of water. Her husband decided they would quickly ford the creek before it got worse, then stay until it had receded again. But when they came near the middle of the creek, they soon saw that it was worse than they had feared. The horses struggled valiantly for footing as the fast-moving current enveloped them. They started swimming, straining to reach the opposite shore, but the power and force of the swift water was too much for them.

The wagon tilted precariously; Magdalena found herself floundering in the muddy, swirling water. She disappeared beneath the surface, then came up sputtering, finding herself being swept downstream. Grabbing desperately for some overhanging branches, she managed to grasp a handful of twigs and was able to hold herself and keep from being swept farther downstream. Her head just above the water, she quickly looked around for her husband. She spied him near the opposite shore, also clinging to overhead branches. The bank was high there and the current much stronger, and he fought desperately to keep from being swept away. They were able to call encouragement to each other above the roar of the water. (They had been swept near a dam where the water rushed over it.) The wagon had lodged on a sand bar and the horses were floundering frantically, but to no avail, for soon the floundering ceased and their heads disappeared beneath the water. Despair settled over the couple as they feared their outcome would be the same.

Magdalena said it seemed as though they were in the raging water for hours, holding on for dear life and hollering for help. The rain and wind had arrived by then, making the situation even more treacherous. The water was still rising.

Just as Magdalena was about to give up all hope, a shout was heard on the bank near her. A man had arrived on the scene and taking in the situation at a glance, quickly ran to get a rope and more help. By the time he returned and a rope was tossed to her, she felt she was nearing unconsciousness. She dimly remembered seeing her husband being swept downstream, then herself catching the rope, but the next thing she remembered was waking up in her bed at home with kind neighbors there to care for her. She was later told that although she had seemed to be unconscious, it had taken two men to pry her hands loose from the rope.

For several days, no one would tell Magdalena anything about her husband, but she knew that he was lost to her forever. It wasn't until his body was found miles downstream that she was told, and then she nearly died, too. It was her little girl, who still needed her mother, and her unborn baby who gave her the will to live. Six weeks after the accident she gave birth to a healthy boy.

For a while Magdalena thought she couldn't go on without her husband, but she somehow found the courage for each new day, and now she will have a help meet again. I think she will make a good wife for Father and will be a good stepmother for our family. She has a very nice personality and is above reproach in her dealings. We don't want to forget our dear mother who loved us and did so much for us, but she is with the angels now, along with little Bessie, and we need someone to help us.

Feronica's Bible verse for this entry was: "Bless the Lord, O my soul: and all that is within me, bless His holy name. Bless the Lord, O my soul, and forget not all His benefits" (Psalm 103:1,2),

October 14

Hal and Mirabelle paid us a visit tonight. Hal was in a storytelling mood and is a very interesting conversationalist. I think I'll relate one of his stories here.

When Hal's grandfather, David, was eleven years old, he had a desire to see the circus. His parents had strictly forbidden him to go, but that didn't lessen his desire to see it. He had heard of trained elephants, dancing bears and monkeys, sword swallowers, and trapeze walkers. So when the circus came to the nearest town, he began to scheme and dream, but he couldn't think of any way he could go without his father finding out.

On the morning of the last day the circus was to be in town, David's father told his son to spend a week at his uncle's place to help with the wheat harvest. He was to walk there since he knew the way, so his dreams received new hope.

David's grandfather had once given him five silver dollars (he had the same name and it was his namesake gift). He got the coins out of the drawer where they had been put for safekeeping and put them in his pocket. When he bade his parents good-bye, he hoped they wouldn't detect the guilty look in his eyes. He planned to spend the day at the circus, then wait until dark to go to his uncle's place and sleep in the barn and pretend he had been sent a day later. There were no telephones in their homes, of course, so he thought he'd be able to pull it off without getting caught.

Hal said that being at the circus was every bit as exciting as his grandfather had thought it would be—at first. He watched all the shows, bought all the candy he wanted, then spent the rest of the time hanging around the tents of the trained animals. When one of the show horses got away from his master, David was the one who caught him and took him back. The man praised him for his quick action, then asked David if he could help with the horses for the rest of the evening, promising him a dollar. David jumped at the chance, and when the man saw that he was used to working with horses and had a way with them, he offered him a permanent job, traveling with the circus.

The salary he promised seemed unbelievable to the young farm boy, and David was tempted above his resistance. He forgot all about his parents, brothers and sisters, and the farm animals at home and gave his word that he would go with the circus. Before quitting time, he had his fortune told by a gypsy lady in a tent. She told him that there was great excitement, prosperity, and fame ahead of him.

When David left the fortune teller's tent, to his dismay he found that he no longer had what was left of his grandfather's five silver dollars, nor the dollar that the trainer had given him.

How the gypsy was able to get them from him without his knowledge was a mystery to him. By that time, he was feeling kind of sick from his revelry throughout the day, but he helped with the packing up and getting everything ready for the train ride to the next town where the circus was scheduled to perform. At the train station he was put into a boxcar with the horses. He was feeling sick and uneasy by then, and as soon as he felt the train beginning to move, the full weight of what he was doing suddenly came crashing down upon him! David realized he might never see his family again, and he realized that he did **not** want to go with the circus after all.

There was a sliding ventilation panel in the boxcar, and David wasted no time. Out of this window he jumped—just in the nick of time before the train began to pick up speed. It was a wonder he didn't fall beneath the train or get his legs crushed, but after he was able to get his breath back again, he was none the worse for jumping.

David found his way to his uncle's barn, and that night he was miserably sick. His conscience smote him, too, and he felt that he was amply rewarded (or punished) for his misdeeds of the day. For a long time he told no one about it, but he did confess it to his parents after a while. I have to wonder what his life would have been like on the road with the circus, and how he would have turned out—certainly not a Christian.

> ***Golden Gem for today:*** *Because we have nothing in ourselves, and God is to be all and do all, our whole attitude should be to look up to Him, expecting and receiving what He is to do. No effort of thy will can bring love. It must be given thee from above.*

October 17

Today I was invited to an all-day quilting at Mom Mullet's house, a good place to catch up on community news. Mom had two quilts in frames—one was a *Weg-Im-Sandt* (Path-in-the-Sand) and the other was a plain white one. I had just finished my housecleaning yesterday, so it was good to have a day of less strenuous work. I hitched a ride over on the pony cart with Jared and Treva, and they picked me up again after school. Kermit spent the day at a sale, so he didn't need to "batch it" today, which was nice.

The weather turned sharply colder today, and we're even having snow flurries. The others are out getting in the last of the corn, so I'll copy some more of Feronica's journal. I had a letter from Great-grandmother Gertrude, and I think she'd like to have the journal back soon, although I'm afraid it will take me several more months before I finish it.

Feronica's next entry was dated December 3:

> Vanity, vanity, all is vanity. "Man is like to vanity: his days are as a shadow that passeth away" (Psalm 144:4). It was on the day after my last entry that misfortune again befell us. Father had borrowed Ulrich's horses and wagon to take all the youngsters to the shoemaker to have their feet measured for new shoes for winter. He was very late this year, and we were sorry they wouldn't be ready in time for the wedding. As it turned out, it was good they weren't ready earlier.
>
> Hans and I had been there on Saturday, so we stayed home. It was such a gorgeous day of Indian summer weather and sunshine, so very rare for this late in the season, that I decided to take my Bible and journal and go for a walk to the creek and sit on a rock, enjoying the beauty of creek and woods.
>
> The golden leaves were floating gently down all around me, and it was all so peaceful. A doe calmly came to the water to drink, and it seemed as if she looked right at me with her alert brown eyes, but didn't seem the least bit alarmed. I heard wild turkeys in the woods and squirrels were darting around in the treetops and coming down for acorns and shellbarks to store for the winter. It was a good feeling to know that our own larder was full and we had plenty of provision, and in a few days, Father would provide us with a stepmother to look after the family.
>
> Hans was out with the axe, clearing away brush and thickets. Next spring they want to fell more trees and clear another field for plowing, for the boys are all growing and will soon need more work. All was so quiet and peaceful that I fell asleep. I don't know how long I slept until the smell of smoke woke me. I quickly jumped up, knowing that a forest fire would be bad

this time of year; it was quite dry and the dried leaves would spread it fast. The Indians often start a fire in the fall to burn off the summer's weeds and their seeds, and sometimes it gets out of hand.

Suddenly, I noticed that the sky had grown dark and a wind had sprung up. Was there a storm coming, or was it smoke?

I ran back to the cabin, shouting for Hans, who was already running toward the cabin. It **was** a forest fire—headed our way!

Soon a lot of men were on the scene, some plowing a wide strip in the field so the fire wouldn't jump across. Others were trying to beat back the fire with wet sacks and shovels. They got the fire stopped, but not before it reached our cabin. Oh, what a helpless

> feeling to see it all go up in flames—our home, Tilda's and my new chintz dresses, and all the other sewing I had done. All the vegetables we had stored in the loft, the big piles of firewood ready for the winter, and the furniture Father had made.
>
> I thought of the verse, "Man is born to trouble as the sparks fly upward—Life is nothing but a vale of tears and sorrows, heartaches and disappointments."
>
> I ran back to the spot where I had sat by the creek, threw myself down on the bank, and cried. There I discovered my Bible and journal where I had left them, and a spark of hope returned to me. I had the Bible, the children were all safe—there was still much to be thankful for, though all that remains of our cabin is some charred embers.
>
> Father and Magdalena were married the next day and we all moved into her house. Her brother and his family had been planning to move there, but now they will build a new house instead. It is not what we had planned, but we want to accept it as God's will.
>
> I haven't yet been able to make myself at home in Magdalena's house, and I feel kind of useless there. I've been thinking maybe I should move away and work for someone else. I must pray for God's leading, but I am so tired. Life seems very tiresome just now and I haven't got much ambition.

There is no flowered Bible verse at the end of this journal entry, and it sounds as if Feronica is trying to ward off discouragement. My heart aches for her and for all the hardships she has already bravely endured. Life surely wasn't easy then, and the early settlers had to be strong in the face of their difficulties.

> **Golden Gem for today:** *Fret not your souls with puzzles that you cannot solve. The solution may never be shown you until you have left this flesh-life. Remember what I have so often told you, "I have yet many things to say unto you, but ye cannot bear them now. Only step-by-step, and stage-by-stage can you proceed in your journey upward. The one thing to be sure is, that it is a journey with Me. There does come a joy known to those who suffer with Me, but that is not the result of the suffering—it is the result of the close intimacy with Me to which the suffering drove you."*

More of Feronica's journal. Her next entry is not until the next spring. She writes:

> May 8—The world is lovely and green once more, and the warm, balmy breezes are back. Everywhere in the woods wildflowers and plants are popping up, the frogs are croaking in the *Schwamm*, and the birds are singing joyously. Wildlife is abundant, the springs are gurgling, and the fern fronds are opening. Meadowlarks and red-winged blackbirds are trilling and dipping down to their nests, robins are singing sweetly, and song sparrows are pouring out their joy to the lovely weather.
>
> Hans and I went to another hymn sing on Saturday evening with Jacob and Lisbet, on horseback. (Timbelman's have the biggest barn, and they always offer to have the gathering there. Everyone likes to go there, so we always have the hymn sing there.)
>
> Horseshoe Trail was muddy after the spring rains, so we cut through the woods as much as we could, where the grass was green and thick, and the footing firm. The swamp just south of Saeue Schwamm Stettle is rather boggy just now and looks like a haven of green for wildlife.
>
> At Timbleman's we sat on benches under the trees to sing, for it was too nice to be inside. The twilight deepened and the stars came out. Soon after we had sung the parting hymn, Yockel came on his black stallion to escort me home. We stopped at our favorite place along the Conestoga. It had been a long time since he'd last gone there because of the long, cold, and snowy winter. We chatted about how it would soon be the time that young people make application to join church. Yockel didn't pressure me to do so, but I know that is what he would like me to do. Yet, why is it so hard to make up my mind? He is a fine young man and would make an excellent husband, so why do I hesitate? Is it the fear of the hardships of our time—the many untimely deaths and the thought of how quickly all that is hoped and planned and dreamed can be swept away, leaving life cheerless and cold?
>
> They say it is better to have loved and lost, than not to have loved at all, so why am I afraid? Would I

be strong enough to see a row of little coffins ready to be put into the ground, half a family wiped out by diphtheria in a few days—a mother's precious babies and children? Or strong enough to see my husband being swept away, never to come back again, as Magdalena did? Or, like Father, who, after months of awaiting a new baby, saw his wife cold and still in death after she hemorrhaged profusely and there was no doctor to be had?

Yockel would very likely ask me to marry him if I would join his church, but I'm just not sure. Just as I was about to say I would join, Yockel held up a hand for silence, gesturing at something on the water. There, not ten feet away, by the light of the moon we saw a canoe come stealthily gliding upstream. Two men were in the canoe—apparently they didn't have a paddle, because they were, as noiselessly as they could, pulling themselves along by the grasses on the banks, by hand.

Just as they came even with us, one man, who was apparently scanning the shore for any sign of danger, gave a startled exclamation, and suddenly leapt from the canoe onto the bank and disappeared into the underbrush. The force of his sudden jump set the canoe rocking dangerously, and it overturned. The other man was thrown into the water with a splash.

Yockel whispered, "Let's get out of here fast." We hadn't gone far when we again startled someone out of a hiding place in the thickets.

We heard a frightened voice say, "Hebbin help me, de slave catcher's after me," as he scuttled off into the deeper thickets.

"A runaway slave," Yockel said, with a sigh of relief. "For awhile there I thought it was robbers. Someone in the area must be helping the slaves to get away from their master. Some hide in the Welsh Mountains, and others are transported to the harbor in Philadelphia. I believe that the Stoners, who live in that big red sandstone house on the Paxton Trail, keep slaves. Maybe it was one of theirs who ran away."

I shuddered as I remembered what Father had seen in Germantown the last time he was there. A slave auction was in progress, and when a black mother and her baby were placed on the block, someone snatched the baby from her arms. The mother wept and pled to have it back, but the curly-haired baby was sold

> separately. The mother's other children were grouped around her, clinging to her and crying, but no mercy was shown. Such a separation would have been worse than the death of a loved one.
>
> The rest of the way home to Magdalena's house was uneventful, and after we had parted at the door, I realized that I had forgotten all about making a commitment to join the Mennonite Church. Later, I was again unsure. I have no desire to be worldly and no wish to be fashionably and proudly dressed. I know it is not the plain Mennonite garb that is holding me back. Yet, maybe it is my selfish pride and self will after all.

Feronica closed her entry with another flower-bordered Bible verse: "Trust in the Lord with all thine heart; and lean not unto thine own understanding. In all thy ways acknowledge Him, and He shall direct thy paths" (Proverbs 3:5,6).

I hope she received the guidance she so sorely needed and was not led astray. I'm afraid that all too often when making decisions, we lean to our own understanding and miss God's best for us.

November 6

Tonight Treva and Jared stayed at the Mullets for supper and then went skating on their big pond in the evening. Yes, we have skating weather now since the temperature turned sharply colder a few days ago. Kermit and I went for a walk in the moonlight, out through the back fields, dodging the few remaining corn shocks, then headed for the creek, past the old range shelter that had been a home to our little campers.

We crossed the creek on the stepping stones and paid a visit to the little house on the other side of the bridge. As we headed up the walk, the door flew open and Mirabelle and Hal welcomed us in, very glad to see us. Mr. Bradford was there, too, so we were glad we had chosen tonight to go.

Mirabelle served us coffee and Krimpets, and Mr. Bradford told interesting stories from his younger days when he was out west working at various projects. We were sorry we couldn't stay longer, but we had to get home and hitch up Patsy to go fetch

Treva and Jared (the pony cart doesn't have lights). As we drove through the darkness with the blinkers flashing, I mentioned to Kermit that I hoped we'd get plenty of snow so that we could go sleighing. He agreed because next winter we might be in Pennsylvania where there isn't as much snow.

At Mullets' pond, someone had built a big bonfire so the skaters could warm themselves, and we sat near it and watched the skaters for awhile. Some were playing "Crack-the-Whip," a few were doing figure eights, and the younger ones were playing tag. The stars were twinkling in the frosty sky and the air was crisp and cold. As we watched the skaters, we marveled at the energy and exuberance of youth and decided that we must be getting old, for the warmth of a fireside was more appealing to us.

Mom Mullet invited us in for spiced cider, and we had a good visit with them until Treva and Jared were ready to go home. We'll have to enjoy these visits with friends while we can, because we'll probably have to move sometime. But we'll make new friends wherever we go, too.

> ***Golden Gem for today:*** *Never weary in prayer. When one day man sees how marvelously his prayer has been answered, then he will deeply, so deeply, regret that he prayed so little. Prayer changes all. Prayer recreates. Prayer is irresistible. So pray, literally, without ceasing.*

November 12

More of Feronica's journal; her next entry was written over five months later, on October 18:

> Magdalena was a schoolteacher before she was first married so she will again be teaching the younger ones their reading, writing, and arithmetic as she did last winter. It's really handy that they don't have to trudge off to school in the winter's snow and cold. Now something has happened that will make it even more handy: six-year-old Jeems has broken his leg.
>
> The boys were gathering shellbarks and walnuts last Saturday near the Mill Creek, and Jeems climbed into the tree to shake down more walnuts. Suddenly, there was a sharp crack and the branch he was on broke, and he fell to the ground. His leg was bent at a grotesque angle, and there was an ugly wound on it—he was in a lot of pain. Instead of coming home with a wagon loaded with walnuts, the boys came pulling their brother.
>
> Father laid him on the kitchen table, and Magdalena gave him a swallow of whiskey to deaden the pain before carefully washing out his wound. When Father stretched out the injured leg to put on a splint, Jeems fainted from the pain. It was a good thing he

did, because he didn't have to suffer while he was unconscious. When he came to again, Jeems still had a lot of pain. Magdalena got some herbs from Granny Oberlein which are supposed to help the pain and fight infection, but he still cries and whimpers. Why must life be so hard? I wish I could understand things better.

Last Saturday I attended Yockel's church again with Jacob and Lisbet, on Fast Day (everyone went without breakfast) and baptismal services—the day the summer class of church applicants was baptized. I felt a bit sad as I watched the young people kneel in front of their bench—sad that I wasn't one of them. The bishop asked the applicants several questions, to which they answered "yes."

It was a very serious and solemn ceremony—a sacred one, for it seemed as if God were near. With a pitcher of water, the minister poured some water into the bishop's hands which were cupped over an applicant's head, then the bishop gave a benediction or blessing as he placed both hands on the person's head. The minister's wife removed each girl's prayer veiling before her turn was reached, then put it back on afterwards and tied the ribbon. The bishop then went back to the first person who was baptized, gave him a hand, helped him to his feet, and greeted him with a holy kiss. The bishop's wife greeted each girl with a holy kiss. They were lifted up to a new beginning, a new life of service to the Lord. As I watched, a great longing filled my heart. I wanted to be baptized, too, and to be a member of the church; I resolved not to put it off any longer. Why had I been so stubborn and hard-hearted for so long?

Jacob, Lisbet, and I were invited to the Timbelman home for dinner after church, and as I saw the love, peace, and harmony in their home, I knew I wanted a home like that, too, and that I wanted Yockel to be the head of that home. I didn't get a chance to talk to Yockel before we started for home, but I wished I could have told him I've made up my mind to join his church. I knew it would make him very happy, and I could just see his face light up with a beautiful, glad smile.

I was very happy all the way home, enjoying the scenery—the colorful leaves on the trees, the golden fall sunshine, the piles of pumpkins which had been gathered from fields dotted with corn shocks, the crowing of pheasants from the fence rows, and the blue,

> blue sky. But when I arrived home, I was greeted with bad news.
>
> Brother Jeems was delirious with a high fever and was tossing and turning. Father said Jeems must have gotten gangrene in his leg, which can be very serious. He sent for a doctor at once, but not the one from Brandywine this time. He sent the Ulrichs to Hickorytown for the new doctor there. At bedtime Magdalena sent me off to bed, saying that she and Father will sit up with Jeems and wait for the doctor. She is a good mother. We all call her Mother, but I still call her Magdalena in my journal.

Feronica's journal entry ends here, again with a flower-bordered Bible verse: "The Lord is my shepherd; I shall not want . . . he leadeth me beside the still waters. He restoreth my soul . . ." (Psalm 23:1-3).

So, she does know where to go for help when life is hard. I'm glad she finally made up her mind to marry Yockel, and I have to wonder why it took her so long to decide. Kermit also thinks she dilly-dallied far too long.

> ***Golden Gem for today:*** *Down through the ages, there have always been those who obeyed, not seeing, but believing, and their faith was rewarded. So shall it even be with you.*

November 16

Our second anniversary has passed, and at last I have some good news to write to my parents! The midwife says that our hopes should be fulfilled in June! It is so much fun planning and dreaming about it, and Kermit is as excited as I am about it. He has bought some woodworking tools and is doing a bit of furniture-making, just as a sideline or hobby. He has already made a beautifully handcrafted and varnished bookcase for me, and now he's working on a mysterious project—something for our nursery, I suppose, but he wants to surprise me.

Love is cherished memories
And sweet dreams come true.

Love is all these precious things
And joy in sharing, too.

November 21

More of Feronica's journal, dated October 28:

The doctor stayed for three days because of Jeems' gangrenous leg. At the end of that time, seeing that Jeems' fever and delirium was getting worse instead of better, he decided that it was time to amputate. Oh, what a shocking verdict. At Father's request, I took the younger ones for a walk down to the Mill Creek. I was thankful that Magdalena was there, doing all she could to assist the doctor. Hans had to stay, and he later told me that it was horrible, hearing the screams. They laid Jeems on the kitchen table to amputate, and there was nothing but whiskey to deaden the pain. It is almost more than my spirit can bear. Why? Why? Why? Why must he be a cripple the rest of his life?

I didn't sleep a wink that night, and in the morning when Lisbet came over she said if I wanted to go along on a trip to Hickorytown, I was welcome to come; they had a horse I could use. I was glad to get away and accepted gladly.

The ride was refreshing, for the day was beautiful. Although it couldn't lift my spirits because of my heartache for Jeems, it did make me feel a little better. Father had given me a bit of money and said I might buy anything I wished that was useful and necessary.

In the little general store in the middle of town, they had everything from dress goods and notions to hardware and foodstuff. There were barrels of little round soda crackers; barrels of pickles in vinegar; barrels of fish in brine; big sacks of flour, cornmeal, and dried beans. I chose material for a black dress, since all the girls who were baptized at Weber's Thal last Saturday were wearing black.

When we came out of the store, we noticed a crowd of people in the town square. In the center, standing on a block of wood, was a small man, preaching to those who were gathered around him. Jacob said that it was Conrad Beissel, founder of the Settlement of the Solitary. I crowded closer, for I've long been fascinated by his teachings, and wanted to hear more. It seemed that when he saw me, Beissel's piercing black eyes looked straight into mine, and I thought he was speaking only to me. I listened spellbound until Lisbet dragged me away. She said she wished she hadn't asked me to come along to Hickorytown, but I was glad to have heard Beissel preach. He seems like a real man of God, and I clung to every word he said and tried to memorize them on the way home.

Life is so hard, so filled with perils and dangers and disappointments. Maybe the Settlement of the Solitary would be a haven of peace and safety—a place to grow spiritual and saintly, away from the allurements of the world. At any rate, I want to find out more about Beissel.

November 22 (Thanksgiving Day)

We were invited to dinner at Pop and Mom Mullet's home, and Mom had roasted a huge home-grown turkey which she had butchered (dressed) and stuffed with filling. It was delicious, as were all the other fixings that went with the feast. We all had much to be thankful for, and we'll cherish the memories of this day after we're no longer living here and can't be with these friends. My thoughts traveled back to Pennsylvania and last Thanksgiving's gathering, and I got *hemveh* for our loved ones there, but we'll be seeing them again soon, Lord willing.

The Mullet girls showed me the quilt they just finished piecing and quilting—a lovely flower garden quilt in all the right shades. I helped the younger ones play a game of Scrabble; then they ran off to go for rides on the pony cart while we visited. Treva and Jared enjoyed the day, too, for they have made a lot of friends here.

I'll copy a verse yet, then, if there's time before Kermit comes in, more of Feronica's journal.

> **Golden Gem for today:** *In everything give thanks, for this is the will of God in Christ Jesus concerning you. Always pray until prayer merges into praise. That is the only note on which true prayer should end.*

More of Feronica's journal; it's date is a month after the last entry, November 29. She wrote:

> Yockel came to see me tonight, and as I saw him tie his black stallion under the forebay, my heart felt as heavy as lead, for tonight I would tell him of my decision. I could hardly bear the thought of his never coming to see me again, but it was what I had made up my mind to do.
>
> It was a chilly evening, but we went for a walk so we could be alone to talk. I told him that on the day of the baptismal services, I had made up my mind to join the Mennonite Church, but now that I had heard Conrad Beissel preaching, I was planning to follow his teachings. It wasn't easy to explain, and I couldn't understand it myself, why I was so gripped by Beissel's words and felt compelled to follow, but so it was. I told Yockel that I was planning to join the Settlement of the Solitary and to stay there the rest of my life.
>
> I felt very heartless when I saw the jolt it gave him, but I knew I had to go through with it even though my heart felt as if it were bleeding. I said that perhaps it was my brother Jeems' misfortune in the loss of his leg that had helped sway me, that and all the other hard things in life—the suffering, pain, loss of loved ones, and many other hardships that are not fair—had helped me to decide to devote my life to spiritual things instead of to a marriage and family.
>
> Yockel tried to explain to me that it was God's will, but I reminded him that there were other girls who would be glad for a chance to marry him. He sadly shook his head. I think he couldn't trust himself to speak, and it nearly broke my heart. It was a bleak evening with the cold wind whipping my skirts, and our hearts were at their bleakest, too. I pled with him to understand why I wanted to dedicate my life to self-denial, greater spirituality, and helping the poor, and that it was more possible in the Settlement of the Solitary than elsewhere. He tried to understand and was very brave, but he was brokenhearted, and that made me feel so bad.
>
> Truly, this life is a vale of tears, sighs, and groans. Heaven must surely be worth it all.

There was no Bible verse at the end of this sad journal entry. Poor Feronica, what will become of her now—I mean, I wonder how she fared at the Ephrata Cloister, as it was later called.

Next week is the big sale day—public sale at Beechwood Acres Farm. Who will the buyer be, and will we have to move?

November 30

I have two very important news items to write, and I'll write the good news first. Ben and Rachel have announced the arrival of an eight-pound son named Vernon! We hitched up and drove right over to see him this afternoon—we couldn't wait any longer! He is the picture of health, red-faced, and squalling; his parents couldn't be happier.

Now for the bad news: Our Beechwood Acres Farm was sold to an outsider and we will have to find somewhere else to move by spring.

In her latest letter, my mother had written about a five-acre property near them that will be available for rent by spring. It's just across the creek from Uncle Nate and Aunt Miriam's home. Kermit and I have been discussing the possibility of renting that, and perhaps he could make a living by having a woodworking shop and planting a few acres of produce, rather than farming. At any rate, we decided to write to Mom and Pop for more information and to see what they think of the idea. I think it would be wonderful living in the old neighborhood again. We'll wait to see what they have to say and keep our eyes open for any other possibilities, such as farms coming up for rent here. I'm sure that something will turn up for us, but in the meantime we'll have to be patient.

Part Four

Winter at Beechwood Acres

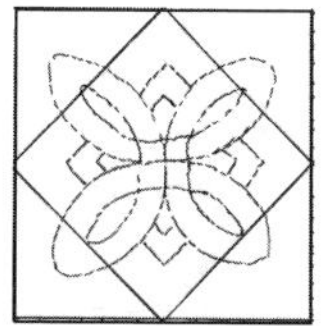

December 1

Beautiful flakes of snow are falling, transforming every tree and bush and all of the landscape into a thing of beauty. Time to get out the big bobsled! Treva and Jared found a string of sleigh bells in the old mill, and although I think that sleigh rides are exhilarating enough without bells jingling, Kermit will humor the youth and put the bells on. Treva and Jared are both invited to a skating party at the Miller's on Saturday afternoon, and Jared wants to put the bells on the pony's harness, too. He'd love to take Patsy and the big bobsled, too, if the roads are still fine for it, but Kermit says he will have to be satisfied with the pony for now.

Kermit and I took the first ride on the bobsled—to town for groceries—and it was so much fun, with the beautiful snowflakes still floating down. Patsy seemed to like it, too. We came home a bit late, but Jared had the chores started and Treva had supper ready. I guess we're spoiled, but it sure was nice. And, to top it off, when it was time for dessert, Treva went to the wash house with a big spoon and bowl and came back with it heaped high with homemade vanilla ice cream. They had made it as a surprise for us. Jared had cut ice out of the little pond and chopped it into bits with the axe, while Treva made the custard. They had taken turns cranking it. It was delicious, topped with chocolate sauce and eaten with big hard pretzels. We will surely miss our *Maad* and *Gnecht* when they leave for home!

Later in the evening when the chores were done, Kermit took Jared and Treva for a ride in the sleigh in the moonlight, and they aren't back yet. This gives me time to copy more of Feronica's journal, but first, another gem.

Golden Gem for today:

God is love—no judging
God is love—no resentment

God is love—all patience
God is love—all power
God is love—all supply

All you need to have is love for God and man. Love for God insures obedience to every wish, every command. Love is the fulfilling of all law. Pray much for love.

More of Feronica's journal. There is no date to this entry:

It is now two years since I came to the Settlement of the Solitary. When I first came here, I was intrigued with the self-denial and found it pleasing to my spirit. I fasted much and prayed continually. I worked in the print shop and in the bakery. I didn't mind sleeping on a narrow hard bench, with a wooden block for a pillow. I helped to distribute bare necessities to the poor and needy. I liked living in the Sister House with other women, helping them with the weaving and making of religious texts in intricate designs. I didn't mind the hard life, kneeling for hours at a time on the cold, hard floor in the House of Prayer. I listened eagerly to Conrad Beissel's teachings, taking in every word and striving to follow them. I felt very holy and spiritual. I had no worries about my younger brothers and sisters, for I knew they were in good hands with Magdalena there to care for them.

My family came to visit me a few times and pled with me to return home with them. It made me feel hard-hearted to refuse, until I had again knelt to pray for hours and fought the battle with self and gotten victory over the flesh once more. Inside the Settlement I felt at peace, away from the storms, sufferings, and uncertainties of life. Being cold, hungry, and worn out from hard work was preferable to that.

But now I'm beginning to feel differently about the place. It's not just a longing to leave—it's a feeling that I should leave. I know that above the door of the Sister House there is an inscription which says:

The house is entered through this door
By peaceful souls who dwell within,
Those who have come will part no more,
For God protects them here from sin.

But I feel as if God is speaking to me, telling me that it is time to go back, leave the Settlement of the Solitary. I will go back to Yockel, and if he will still have me, I will marry him. I will tell him how often I missed him, longed for him, and prayed for him. I realized I loved him after I was in the Settlement but was swayed too much by Beissel's powers to leave. I will be the joyful mother of children, and if God

> chooses to take them away after He has given them, I will say, "The Lord hath given, the Lord hath taken away, blessed be the name of the Lord." I will cheerfully endure the hardships, danger, and uncertainties of life outside the Settlement. I shall go tonight before I lose courage.

Once more Feronica had copied a Bible verse bordered with flowers: "In Thy presence is fulness of joy; at thy right hand there are pleasures for evermore" (Psalm 16:11).

December 25

After several weeks of the flurry of cookie baking, candy making, and gift wrapping, all seems rather quiet and peaceful around here today. I was afraid we'd have a green (or brown) Christmas because our last snow had all melted. But yesterday big, fluffy flakes of white snow came swirling down, rather slowly at first. Soon they became smaller and came down faster and faster, and by evening the snow was so deep I was afraid our guests wouldn't be able to come.

But this morning the sun shone on the lovely snow-covered fields, trees, and woods, and the roads were excellent for sleighing. We had invited Pop Mullet and Ben, Rachel, and Baby Vernon. They all came, rosy-cheeked from their cold rides. I didn't have a turkey to roast, but Kermit had bought a big capon which we had kept in the freezer locker until now. Everyone said it was every bit as good as turkey would have been. It did taste good, stuffed with bread filling and giblets.

It was an enjoyable day, but, of course, my thoughts traveled back to the loved ones at "home" and to the gathering they'd be having, and that we weren't able to be there. But the sadness was quickly gone when I remembered there is a possibility we might be moving to Pennsylvania in the spring.

Pop Mullet read the Christmas story and we all chimed in to sing a few Christmas carols. All too soon it was time for them to bundle up for their cold rides home.

Later this evening Kermit hitched Patsy to our one-horse sleigh, and we went for a ride, enjoying the tingling cold air under the starry skies, while covered with carriage robes. All in all, it was a joyous Christmas with lots to be thankful for and many blessings to count.

Joy to the world! The Lord is come,
Let earth receive her King.
Let every heart, prepare Him room,
And Heaven and nature sing!

December 27

Feronica's next journal entry doesn't have a date either:

> I am at home in Father and Magdalena's house and glad to be here. I couldn't believe how good supper tasted! We had sizzling sausages almost covered by heaps of potatoes, dried corn in cream, turnips cooked in beef broth, and pickled beans. Wild honey dripped from thick slabs of bread, and after all that was eaten, Magdalena passed steaming cups of meadow tea and great wedges of apple pie.
>
> Hans is a strapping young man by now, and Tilda is a demure young lady. I hardly know my little broth-

ers anymore, and Magdalena's daughter and son even less. Father and Magdalena have added two more children to their family since I left and have built an addition to the house last year. I now have to wonder what strange thing motivated me to leave for the Settlement of the Solitary—it is so good to be free! I want to help Magdalena and Tilda with the work here for awhile, but first I must go to see Yockel—tomorrow if the weather is good. I am very anxious to go. How could I have hurt and disappointed him so? He is such a fine person.

Tonight when the boys came in for supper, it was a jolt to me to see Jeems come in on crutches, his one pant leg hanging empty. But he was as smiling and jolly as the rest, and I was reminded of what Jesus said, "My grace is sufficient for thee."

It seems to me that life is good after all, here in the Conestoga Valley. Tilda told me that the Ulrich's barn burned six weeks ago, and people came from far and near, bringing food, lumber, and whatever they could spare, and in a short time a new barn was built. That's real kindness and neighborliness and I want to be a part of it, too.

Tomorrow I'll go see Yockel, then I'll help with cooking apple butter in the big copper kettle, the baking of the many loaves of bread it takes for hungry growing boys, the butchering, harvesting of crops, and preserving of the summer's bounties. I want to help prepare the flax for the spinning wheel and prepare the sheep's soft fleece for weaving and spinning. And then, if Yockel is still willing, we'll be married in November.

Feronica's verse for this entry was: "Show us Thy way, O Lord, and let us walk in Thy paths. Lead us in Thy truth and teach us."

January 1

A brand new year, and a new opportunity to serve the Lord with all our hearts, souls, and minds. Mirabelle and Hal were here today, bringing Mr. Bradford and a big pot of pork and sauerkraut. Delicious! Mirabelle even put a few stitches in the quilt I had in the frame, a Log Cabin quilt in shades of blue. They couldn't stay long after dinner—as soon as the dishes were done they left, but then we had another surprise!

Another car came in the drive, bringing our happy little campers, Chet, Diane, and Billy! They brought some belated Christmas gifts for us. All three of them appear to be the picture of health and happiness, so they must like living with their aunt.

Billy wanted to make a snowman, so they all donned their boots and ran outside to play. While they were outside, their aunt told us more about the children's stepfather. Shortly after the children had left home, he was diagnosed with having a brain tumor which affected his personality. He has had surgery to remove the tumor, and the doctors were able to get it all, and now he's fine again. He wants the children back again, but they're going to finish their school term where their aunt lives. We talked about the bravery of the children sleeping in the range shelter on the island and doing their own cooking and washing. I suppose the Lord's protecting hand was over them.

> ***Golden Gem for today:*** *The secure, immovable life of My disciples is not built at a wish, in a moment, but is laid, stone by stone, foundation, walls, and roof, by the acts of obedience, the daily following of My wishes, the loving doing of My will.*

January 2

I'll take the time to copy more of Feronica's journal while Kermit is shoveling snow. She doesn't bother to use dates anymore, but she does say that it is lovely weather. She writes:

> My heart is very sad and heavy tonight, but I'll try to write what happened today.
>
> I started out early this morning for the Timbelman's home. It was a beautiful morning with wildflowers blooming along Horseshoe Trail, and mourning doves cooed from a treetop. A pair of cardinals whistled from a pine tree, and my spirits matched their joyful song, and I hummed a happy tune. Bunnies scampered away, bobwhites called from

the thickets, a graceful deer leapt over a stump, crashed into the underbrush, and disappeared.

Near Weber's Thal I stopped to chat with my Indian friends and was reminded of the blue beads an Indian girl had once given to me. I knew I couldn't wear them if I joined the Mennonites, so I gave them to Tilda, not realizing I would be joining the Settlement of the Solitary instead.

At the Timbelman's farm, I was surprised to find that they had built a new stone house near the old one. It was three or four times larger than the old one and contained a second story and had many windows. I strained my eyes to see if I could get a glimpse of Yockel anywhere, possibly working in the field somewhere with the horses, and I wondered if he still had his black stallion. But there was no one to be seen, so I went to the door of the old house and knocked. A young woman with a child on her arm answered the door, and I stared in amazement.

"Lisbet!" I cried. "Wh—what are you doing here?"

"Feronica!" she cried in return. "Please come in! It's been so long since I've seen you. Have you left the Settlement of the Solitary?"

I explained it all to her and she nodded understandingly. She said, "We were praying for you and hoped you would come back soon. And now our prayers are answered."

"I came to see Yockel," I told her. "Do you know if he is at home?" It still hadn't occurred to me why Lisbet would be there.

"Yes," she said slowly, looking intently and a bit anxiously into my eyes. "Yes, my husband Yockel is at home, working in one of the back fields."

Her words stunned me at first, and I sat down on the chair she had offered me. "Your **husband** Yockel?" I repeated dazedly. "You married Yockel?"

Lisbet nodded, "Last November."

I looked at the little girl in her arms. "Then this isn't your child?"

Lisbet shook her head. "No, this is my brother Jacob's daughter, Becky. Her mother, Yockel's sister Rebecca, died a year ago when Becky was born."

It was all too much for me to comprehend. Why hadn't anyone told me? Why hadn't I thought to ask before I started out? Lisbet married to Yockel! And

Jacob had been married to Rebecca, who was in her grave for a year already.

I stayed for an hour or so, but our visit was strained, no longer like the old happy times. I didn't want to stay until Yockel came into the house, so I began the long walk back home. The day had started so bright and hopeful, but now I was sad and discouraged.

> I stopped at the place near the Conestoga Creek where Yockel and I used to visit, and I threw myself down on the carpet of grass, weeping as the memories and regret washed over me. There was no one to blame but myself. I lay there in the shady, fern-surrounded dell until at last I had won the victory and found peace again. I would accept this as God's will, I resolved, and try to be a blessing to others, just as Hans Graf's first wife had done when she came to America and discovered that her husband had another wife and a family. I certainly had no claim to Yockel whatsoever and it was foolish of me to suppose that he was still single.

Feronica's Bible verse for the day was: "The Lord is nigh unto them that are of a broken heart; and saveth such as be of a contrite spirit" (Psalm 34:18). She also added: "A broken and contrite heart, O God, thou wilt not despise" (Psalm 51:17b).

January 3

An old-fashioned blizzard is howling outside over our Beechwood Acres farm, flinging drifts of snow into every nook and cranny. Treva and Jared didn't go to school today because the snow was already deep this morning and hasn't let up since. If this continues all night, we'll be snowbound for a few days. Kermit once again said that we might as well enjoy a blizzard in Montana while we can, since this winter might be the last opportunity to do so for quite awhile. We might be moving to Pennsylvania! Treva is embroidering quilt top patches, and I am quilting. Kermit and Jared are working in the little makeshift woodworking shop, putting together small projects for a craft store.

Later—as I wrote those last words, we were startled to hear an urgent knock on the porch door. *Now who would be out in such stormy weather, braving the blizzard winds*, I wondered. Kermit flung open the door, and there, huddled together and shivering, stood a man and a boy, looking like snowmen, covered with a powdery coating of snowflakes.

Kermit gave them a hearty welcome, saying, "Come in out of the cold and storm and close the door—it feels like it could be zero degrees out there."

"Thank you, I believe we will accept your offer," the man said politely. "The boy here is shivering with cold. Our car got stuck in a snowdrift out on the road near your barn. Would you mind—uh, I hate to ask, but if we could somehow get it under a roof somewhere, we could make out."

"Of course!" Kermit reached for his overcoat, cap, and boots, and Jared did the same. "I'll hitch up the horses, and we'll get it out of the drift in a jiffy. I'll open the barn doors, and you can drive right in."

While they were gone, Treva helped the boy take off his snowy-hooded jacket. The cookstove was glowing red with heat, radiating its warmth all over the kitchen, and the boy stretched out his hands to warm them. Treva put the boy's wet mittens on the pipe shelf and hung his jacket on the hook behind the stove."Now you'll soon be thawed out," she told him cheerfully. "You'll be toasty warm in a jiffy."

"Thank you," the boy said gratefully. "My name is Bobby, and my uncle's name is George. I'm glad we got stuck near your farm. Maybe tomorrow I can see the animals. I'd like that."

"We'll be glad to show them to you," Treva said as she gave him the cup of hot chocolate that I had prepared. "Maybe you can even help with the chores."

When the men came in, stamping the snow off their boots, the boy's Uncle George said, "C'mon, Bobby, I guess we'd better head for our bed out in the car. Maybe we can borrow some blankets from these folks."

But, of course we wouldn't hear of it. We have two spare bedrooms, and George seemed relieved that we insisted they use them. Treva made popcorn, and Jared brought a bowl of apples up from the cellar. Before the evening was over, we had made new friends. George said that he grew up on a farm and we were to be sure to wake him and Bobby early enough to help with the chores. The wind was still howling and the snow was coming down as fast as ever when bedtime arrived, and I was thankful for our chests filled with extra blankets, quilts, and comforters.

January 4

The blizzard had stopped by morning, but the snow was more than three feet deep and the drifts much higher. We didn't have to wake George and Bobby; they were up bright and early and bundled themselves up in the extra clothing we loaned them. They waded the drifts to the barn, following Kermit and Jared who led the way with lanterns. Treva and I went out a bit later, and brrr! was it ever cold! Inside the barn, it was warm, cozy, and pleasant. Bobby loved it, and George said it brought back so many memories for him—the welcoming nickering of the horses; the low mooing of the cows as they waited for their breakfast; the cats rubbing against our legs, hungry for their morning milk; the banties waking up on their roosts above the stables and clucking cheerfully, as one by one they flew down.

Bobby watched as I milked Brindle and was highly amused when I squirted some at a hungry cat waiting nearby. He fell utterly in love with our fluffy pup and begged his uncle to be allowed to buy him. George reminded him that no one had said that the pup was for sale. But Kermit told him that we might be moving to Pennsylvania in the spring, and if Bobby wanted the pup, we would be glad to let him have it. So Bobby was one happy boy when his uncle promised to bring him back in March to pick up the pup.

At the breakfast table, George again talked about his memories when we passed the platters of fried cornmeal mush, eggs, *ponhaus*, fried potatoes, and pancakes dripping with syrup. He declared that it could be hard on his cholesterol count, but that didn't keep him from taking second helpings.

When the sun rose, it sparkled on a world of whiteness, drifts, swirls, and snow-covered bushes. It was the deepest snow we had all winter, and we knew, from our previous snows, that it could take a few days until the snowplows found their way to our neck of the woods. So our guests prepared themselves for a long visit. But then, close to lunchtime, several snowmobilers were circling around our place, using the farm fields as a driving course. George wondered out loud whether one of them could possibly take them home. So Kermit flagged down one of them when they came close to the house, and they agreed to take our guests home, a distance of about five miles. I suppose it was a good thing they did, because it was three or four days before they could have gone home in their car, and then we soon had more snow. George and Bobby said they enjoyed being stranded with us and will return later for the car.

Ya well, it's bedtime, and Kermit is coming in from shoveling still more snow, and there's time for a verse yet.

> **Golden Gem for today:** *Think how a smile, or word of love, goes winged on its way—a God-Power, simple though it may seem, while the mighty words of an orator can fall fruitless to the ground. The test of all true work and words is—are they inspired by love?*

January 5

More of Feronica's journal. Again, her entry has no date; it only says that it was written five years after her last entry. She must have lost interest in journal writing, or was too busy. She writes:

> I came across this old journal in a chest, while looking for something else, and sat down to re-read it. I was moved to tears as I read of the hard times, the times of indecision, and how often I made the wrong choices. These past five years have been happy ones though, as I filled my life with working and doing for others what I could. I've enjoyed living with Midwife Molly, as everyone calls her, up here on the Lookout, and being a helper to her. The old Indian trail over the hill where we live has been named *"Katze Boucle"* path, which is German for Cat's Back, because climbing the hill is much like climbing a cat's back. The view is tremendous up here, especially when the leaves are off the trees, for the surrounding wooded hills and valleys make a scenic picture.
>
> I suppose Molly chose to build her home up here because of the rugged beauty and loftiness, and she has always been an independent woman. She owns half a dozen good, sure-footed horses on which we travel to the places where we are summoned to attend birthings.

I have been Molly's assistant for long enough now that I can manage by myself when there are two births at the same time, although she is still more skilled and experienced than I am. It is a wonderful job, being witness to the miracle of birth and a part of the joy and gladness of hearing the first lusty cry of the newborn. But there are still too many cases where we are at a loss to know what to do and powerless in the face of complications. The hard part of our job is when the baby dies, and harder still when the mother dies. Molly says that someday we will have the knowledge and wherewithal to do away with these things.

And so often we are helpless in the face of childhood diseases; the graveyards are full of the graves of little children. The heartbroken parents must go on without them. So we rejoice when all is well—the baby plump and healthy, the mother feeling well—and we hope that the babies will grow up to be fine Christian men and women, a blessing to mankind and the world they are born into.

There are so many changes coming to our new land here in America. More roads are being surveyed, and some are heading westward on the road to Harris Ferry and beyond. Sometimes I feel restless, longing for the chance to travel, even if it's out into the wilderness to open new frontiers, on to new adventures and experiences. I guess I was stifled too long in the confines of the Settlement of the Solitary. Conrad Beissel still has many followers, and his print shop is thriving. Many, like me, leave again after a few years, but there are always others to take their places. I am not sorry for the time I spent there and the lessons in self-denial and humility I learned there.

She concluded her entry with another flower-bordered Bible verse, just as she had when she wrote regularly: "Hereby perceive we the love of God, because He laid down His life for us: and we ought to lay down our lives for the brethren. But whoso hath this world's good, and seeth his brother have need, and shutteth up his bowels of compassion from him, how dwelleth the love of God in him?" (1 John 3:16-17).

January 6 (Sunday)

Today we attended church services at Ben's, and the realization that soon we will be leaving our friends for Pennsylvania tugged at our heartstrings. They seem dearer as we close our eyes to the little faults and imperfections which everyone has in one way or another. It is fairly certain now that we will be moving to the place near Uncle Nate and Aunt Miriam's home.

According to their letters, Mom, Pop, and the whole family are eagerly looking forward to seeing us move closer. And who knows, maybe we'll like it so well there that we'll never want to move back! I hope we get a chance to see our Tall Cedars Homestead once again before we leave, as well as Mrs. Bryan and Bethany, and maybe even Emily and her baby brother.

Kermit refilled the bird feeder yesterday, and now I see chickadees, a bright red cardinal and his mate, a tufted titmouse, and a nuthatch waiting their turn to dart in for sunflower seeds. There is so much we will miss when we move, but we'll still have the memories.

> ***Golden Gem for today:*** *Duty faithfully done for Me means entrance into a life of joy—My joy, the joy of your Lord. The world may never see it, the humble, patient service, but I see it, and My reward is not earth's fame, earth's wealth, earth's pleasures, but the joy divine.*

January 11

Between taking cookies out of the oven and refilling the pans, I'll copy more of Feronica's journal. This entry was written two years after the last one, which shows that she wasn't really into journal writing anymore until an important event took place. She was asked for her hand in marriage by a widower with nine children! (I couldn't resist reading on ahead.)

She writes:

> Once more I'll take my pen in hand to make an entry in the journal I've neglected so long. It's autumn, the sumac is crimson on the vine, and the wild geese

are winging their way overhead, and the golden leaves are falling from the trees. The frost lays heavy and white on the landscape every morning, and the fields are dotted with pumpkins and corn shocks. Flocks of wild turkeys are roosting every evening here in the trees in the Lookout, and the pheasants are crowing in the fields.

This morning two men came at the same time with requests for us to attend to birthings at their homes—one several miles northeast of Weber's Thal, and one in Earltown. That meant we couldn't go together. I chose the one in Earltown, so Molly left for the longer ride. It was a brisk morning. As I saddled my horse to head for Earltown, I heard approaching hoofbeats.

At the foot of Katze Boucle Path, I met the rider coming up, and I thought, *Oh, no! Not another woman giving birth just when we're both needed elsewhere.* But when he came closer, I saw that it was Minquas Tom (so named because he lives on the Great Minquas Path), whom I knew slightly from the birthings we had attended at his house. I knew he did not need a midwife, because his wife had died several years ago and his aunt was keeping house for him and caring for the little ones. He stopped his horse abreast of me and took off his hat and bowed politely, revealing a full head of bushy black tresses. I remember thinking that his flowing black beard and moustache nearly concealed his features, but his eyes revealed much. He appeared to be a bit nervous as he asked in which direction I was heading, then asked if he could ride along since he wished to speak to me.

At first, as we rode along, we spoke only of common things, such as the weather, the changes taking place in the Conestoga Valley, and of the bountiful harvest we had this season. But then he fell silent, and after no one had spoken for nearly a half-mile, he bared the intentions of his heart to me—he wanted to ask for my friendship. He did not speak of marriage, although he did mention that his aunt was getting older and that his children were in need of a mother's care.

I knew that the friendship was to lead to marriage, and the thought of it was so sudden and shocking to me that I couldn't answer right away.

When I found my voice, I told him that I wanted time to think it over, and that he could come to the Lookout on Sunday evening, and I would give him my answer. He said that this was fair—I could have all the time I needed to decide. We parted before we reached Earltown, with him heading south on Peter's Road.

I wonder if he realized how he had left my heart all in a whirl of conflicting thoughts and feelings. I felt dazed, and my feelings kept churning from one viewpoint to the other. First, amazement and gladness, then doubts and dread and shrinking away from the idea. It would be a great undertaking with so many children to clothe and feed, and I knew that Minquas Tom was not well-to-do. He didn't own any land, and his cabin was crude—a far cry from the stone houses most people of any means were building nowadays. I was aware of the hardships and deprivation I would be letting myself in for, yet I knew those children needed a mother, and that I could choose to fill that need.

At Earltown, I delivered a healthy baby boy to a beaming Mennonite mother, and I thought of Yockel and all he had once offered me. He and Lisbet have done well on the piece of land bequeathed to them near his father's farm, and they now own over 300 acres and have a fine family. But I quickly put those thoughts out of my mind, for I knew that I had done what I thought was right at the time, and that I should not dwell on the regrets. I had resolved to accept it as God's will, and I knew that He could bless my life in another way He had chosen for me.

The more I thought about it, the more I began to feel that it was God's will for me to say "yes" to Tom, and I knew that He would not let us starve; He would provide for our needs if not our wants. I did not think much about love—at the time I could not grasp the idea that eventually love would grow in our marriage, and that love would make every burden light.

Feronica's flower-bordered Bible verse for that day's entry was: "Lead me in Thy truth, and teach me: for Thou art the God of my salvation; on Thee do I wait all the day" (Psalm 25:5).

January 12

I received a letter yesterday from Great-grandmother Gertrude, and that reminded me that I must finish copying Feronica's journal soon because I want to mail it back to her before we move. I'll copy more of it now. Feronica's next entry was in the spring. She writes:

> The woods here on the Lookout are greening, the grass is becoming thick and green, and the skunk cabbages are popping up in the hollow. Birds are singing everywhere, and the weather is balmy.
>
> In just two weeks from today Tom and I will be married! I have my wedding dress sewn, and Mother Magdalena has made me a new bonnet. The wedding will be here at Molly's, then after I am gone, my sister Tilda will take my place being Molly's assistant. Tom has been able to purchase two heavy work horses and a big canvas-covered wagon, and we, with our family, plan to start on our trip westward the day after the wedding, taking the road that leads to Harris Ferry and for many miles beyond, where land is cheaper. It will be hard work clearing the land and carving out a productive homestead for ourselves, but it will be a good place for the children to grow up, away from worldly influences.
>
> We hope to be able to wrest a living from the wilderness, if we work hard and are willing to make sacrifices. There will be dangers and hardships, but God will be with us; He has promised to never leave us nor forsake us. It is a good thing that I learned to fight hard battles with self, there on the cold, hard floor in the House of Prayer in the Settlement of the Solitary. I am sure that I will struggle for the victory many times, on my knees in the wilderness. I hope and pray that I can be an help meet for Tom and a good mother to his children, leading them in the path of righteousness—the narrow road that leads to Heaven's gates at the end.

Feronica copied part of the twenty-third Psalm and encircled it with flowers: "The Lord is my shepherd; I shall not want. He maketh me to lie down in green pastures: He leadeth me beside the still waters. He restoreth my soul: He leadeth me in the paths of righteousness for His name's sake" (Psalm 23:13).

Her next entry was three weeks later, when the wedding was over and they were traveling by wagon to their new home in the wilderness. She writes:

> We've been traveling for nearly a week now and are getting used to life on the trail. Harris Ferry is a big place, bustling with activity. The Susquehanna River is even wider than I imagined it to be—we were all awed by its majesty and beauty. The sun sparkled on the rippling water, and the tree-covered mountains made a scenic background.
>
> Four-year-old Tommy shouted, "I see the ocean. Is it the ocean, Papa?"
>
> Twelve-year-old Maria had been telling him about the big ships that sail on the Atlantic, bringing passengers from Europe. Traveling across the Susquehanna on the big ferry was an exciting experience for the children.
>
> We are now traveling through wooded country. Cooking over a campfire hasn't been too bad because we've had dry weather—sunny, breezy days and pleasant temperatures. I'll be glad when we arrive, though, and have a cabin to sleep in again. Tom is a kind, good-natured father and the children love and respect him. I hope I can be the type of mother to them that I should be, and a blessing to the family.

Feronica's verse for this entry was: "My presence will go with thee, and I will give thee rest" (Exodus 33:14). It was encircled with a border of tiny hearts this time instead of flowers.

January 17

Treva and I have been packing things we don't need on a daily basis, in order to work ahead a bit. Thankfully, there's not all that much to do since we had only furnished part of the house. Yesterday one of Treva's friends came here after school and stayed the evening with us and overnight, then went to school with Treva and Jared on the pony cart this morning.

We made two batches of doughnuts. I had the dough all ready when they came home, and soon the kitchen was filled with the delicious aroma of the yeasty, golden brown cakes. Treva dipped half of them in powdered sugar, and we filled the rest with cream filling. I think the wonderful aroma must have traveled across the fields to Hal and Mirabelle's house (just joking), for they soon appeared at the door for an evening visit, and we sent them home later with a box of doughnuts.

We'll surely miss our good neighbors, but I keep thinking that we'll come back to this area again sometime, perhaps to find a place to live in this neighborhood. We're hoping another farm will come up for rent just when we need it. (Smiles)

I received a letter today from my friend Rosabeth. She told me a lot of school stories—the cute sayings and antics of the little first graders, and the funny and interesting things some of the pupils wrote in their compositions. It all brought back so many dear memories of when I was in school. It's good to know that the children are in good hands. (Rosabeth is a born teacher and somehow brings out the very best in them.) She would make someone a very good wife, too, if God so wills it.

> ***Golden Gem for today:*** *Seek in every way to become childlike. Seek, seek, seek until you find, until the years have added to your nature that of the trusting child. Not only for its simple trust must you copy the child's spirit, but for its joy in life, its ready laughter, its lack of criticism, its desire to share all with men. Ask often that ye may become as little children, friendly and loving towards all—not critical, not fearful. Except ye become as little children, ye cannot enter the kingdom of Heaven.*

January 19

While Kermit is finishing the chores, I'll take the time to copy more of Feronica's journal. Her next entry is in the fall, after they've built their house and are settled in their new home in Buffalo Valley. She writes:

> Once more I take my pen in hand to fill an entry in my journal. We have had another bountiful year and

have much to be thankful for. We have a sturdy, well-built cabin, a barn, and a spring house. Our neighbors, the Rudys and the Moyers, have been a big help to us; without their help we could not have managed. We have plenty stored away for the winter: potatoes, turnips, squash, and three fat hogs in the barn, ready to be butchered. Deer and bears are plentiful in this area and Tom is a good marksman, so we need not go hungry.

The children are all well, healthy, and growing. Tom is a good, kind husband, and though we have no luxuries, we are happy and content. Tom and the boys have a trap line, and we're hoping that with the money we make selling the fur, we can buy more land on which to keep the boys busy. So, we're hoping for a good fur year, but we'll take it as it comes.

Her Bible verse for the day was: "It is a good thing to give thanks unto the Lord, and to sing praises unto Thy name, O most High: to shew forth Thy lovingkindness in the morning, and thy faithfulness every night" (Psalm 92:1-2).

Just two weeks later, Feronica had another entry in her journal. She wrote:

In my entry of two weeks ago, I was counting our blessings and perhaps feeling too high and lifted up, and maybe not giving God the honor and glory that I should have. I was brought low a week later when a terrible calamity happened. Little Tommy wandered off alone into the woods. Maria and I were knotting a comforter and did not know he had run after his father and brothers on the trap line. Neither did they know he was following. When Tom and the boys came back it was nearly dark, but they found his footprints leading into the woods. They quickly lit lanterns and searched the woods, calling for Tommy as they went. I knelt by my bed and prayed that if it was the Lord's will, Tommy's life would be spared. They called and searched all night, knowing that savage beasts of prey prowled the woods, but there was no answer.

They found him in the morning, too late to save Tommy from the big grey wolf that had found him just moments before. They shot the wolf, and now our hearts lie broken and bleeding, wondering why God

> could not have seen fit to let Tom and the boys get there just a few minutes earlier. But it is not for us to question why.
>
> All that first day, the longing to run back into the Settlement of the Solitary held me in its grip—the longing to run away from the vulnerability of life with its pain and sorrows. But, that evening I remembered that long ago, when I decided to go back to Yockel, I had decided that if God gave me children, then later took them back unto Himself, I would still praise Him and say, "The Lord hath given, the Lord hath taken away, blessed be the name of the Lord."

Feronica added these Bible verses, without the usual border of flowers and hearts: "Though [God] slay me, yet will I trust in Him" (Job 13:15a). And, "My grace is sufficient for thee" (II Corinthians 12:9a).

February 1

Feronica's last journal entry was so sad—she had yet another hardship to bear. But her spark of courage at the end was inspiring. She had found the strength to face the hard things in life, though she admits that at first, the desire to hide in the Settlement of the Solitary had come back. But that is very understandable under the circumstances.

Treva and Jared have left us rather suddenly and unexpectedly—an aunt of theirs died, and a van load from here went to the funeral. So now it seems rather lonely around here. But it won't be long until we leave for Pennsylvania. We can't help but feel excited about it.

Last evening we had unexpected visitors: our snowbound friends, Bobby and his Uncle George, stopped in. Someone dropped them off to get the car. Bobby hugged Fluffy, the pup, as if he were a long-lost friend, but he won't be able to take the pup along after all. A friend gave him a Dalmatian puppy for his birthday. So I guess Fluffy goes to Ben and Rachel after all. Bobby cried about it, though, and I wish he could have taken the puppy with him.

The Mullets are having church on Sunday, and I'm glad for a chance to visit them before we leave. We're invited to stay for supper, and we're looking forward to it.

Golden Gem for today: *Keep the eye of your spirit ever upon Me. You have ever to know that all things are yours—that what is lovely I delight to give you.*

February 2

We are having some unseasonably mild weather, and it almost gives me spring fever. I even saw some daffodil shoots poking out of the ground near the mill.

And now for the last entry in Feronica's journal. It was written in the springtime, after Tommy had died. She wrote:

> The dogwood trees are budding, and the loveliness of springtime is here again. I am lying in bed as I write this, and Maria is sitting on the rocker holding Baby Julia, who was born yesterday. The baby has big, dark eyes, a dusting of dark hair, and a tiny button nose. Maria declares she's the cutest baby she has ever seen! Tom says she favors his sister Hilda, who died when she was a little girl. Having tasted the joys of motherhood, I marvel anew at the awesome miracle of birth, and at the responsibility of bringing up a soul in the nurture and admonition of the Lord. I am too weak to write more, so I'll lay this aside until later.

Those were the last words she had written in her journal. At the bottom of the page someone had written that Feronica had died one year later. It does not say why she died. There is nothing more, except on the last page there is a list of home remedies for different ailments. I'll copy that here, too.

1. *Soak red flannel in hot tallow and bind it around the neck for sore throat.*
2. *Tie bacon fat on cuts and sores to draw out infection.*
3. *Eat boiled onions and sugar to cure a cold.*
4. *Tie a rag soaked in a mixture of soap and vinegar on a painful boil to cure it.*
5. *Dog fat is a remedy for rheumatism.*
6. *A wool string tied around a finger will stop nosebleed.*
7. *Onion poultices tied to the soles of the feet should cure a fever.*

- from the *Almanac*

I wish Feronica had written more in the last year of her life, or that little Julia would have added more when she was old enough. For Julia also eventually became a great-great-(one less "great" than Feronica) grandmother to me. I am sorry to have this journal come to an end, but am thankful for all she did write, and I hope to pass it on to my children and grandchildren someday. I'll wrap it carefully and mail it to Great-grandmother Gertrude.

Time for bed, because we want to go to Ben and Rachel's to help with the butchering tomorrow.

February 11 (Sunday)

Winter is back again, with more beautiful snow covering our Beechwood Acres Farm's every imperfection and flaw. It looks like a picture postcard now, but of course it won't last. I felt a twinge of sadness when I thought of the apple and pear trees blooming in May, the rose bushes covered with fragrant crimson blooms, and the honeysuckles blooming on the meadow bank, and our not being here to enjoy it.

We were at church at the Mullet's today and heard an inspiring sermon. It was good visiting with all the church folks again, and it brought back many a memory of our few years in Montana. We stayed for supper, and in the evening we sat and reminisced about old times; then we sang hymns until it was time for us to leave. (I guess we'll call that our farewell singing.) We'll sure miss all the folks in this community, but Kermit said on the way home that we'll be back, Lord willing. He quoted:

Make new friends—keep the old;
The one is silver—the other is gold.

Both are precious and needed.

> **Golden Gem for today:** *Though My way may seem a narrow way, it yet leads to Life, abundant Life. Follow it. It is not so narrow but that I can tread it beside you. It's never too lonely with such companionship. A comrade infinitely tender, infinitely strong, will tread the way with you.*

March 5

This is the last page of my journal, and Mom has sent me a new one to fill. It will be a fitting place to begin a new one (at a new chapter in our lives—living in Pennsylvania, and then parenthood in June). I have to wonder if I'll have the time and inclination to do much writing though, when there is a new baby to rock and cuddle and love.

My once-lovely kitchen looks bare and empty, and so do the other rooms. Everything has been packed, and my eyes keep filling with tears. Fluffy is with Ben and Rachel, and Patsy is sold to the Mullets, so we'll have to find ourselves a new dog and horse when we get to Pennsylvania.

We'll be leaving tomorrow morning, along with a vanload of other travelers. The truck containing our household goods and everything else we'll need is already loaded, with the help of good friends and church folks. We're thankful that the roads are good for traveling and that no major blizzards are predicted. Hal and Mirabelle came to say good-bye, and even Mrs. Elegant came with a farewell gift. Yesterday afternoon our church folks surprised us by having a farewell hymn-sing at the Mullet's, and we were presented with a gift of a beautiful quilt, which consisted of a lot of beautiful patches, all hand made by friends and relatives, with their names embroidered on it. It's a lovely keepsake, too special for everyday use, so we'll keep it on the spare bed.

Kermit and I went for a walk tonight, enjoying the beauty and the peacefulness of the evening. A song sparrow trilled from a fence row, and the sunset was splendid. It's rather had to believe that we'll soon be so far away and living in a new home.

This afternoon we hired a driver and visited Chuck at the Tall Cedars Homestead. He was really glad to see us, and that place brought back so many memories. Beechwood Acres Farm holds a lot of precious memories, too, but I'm sure we'll make new ones in Pennsylvania. We stopped at the post office, and I mailed Great-grandmother Gertrude's journal to her.

Yes, a chapter of our lives is closing, and a new one, clean and unspoiled, lies before us. I think it would be fitting to copy a prayer out of my *Prayer Book for Earnest Christians* in the closing of this journal:

> *Father, You alone are wise. Not only do You live in the light, but You Yourself are the eternal light. We are living here in this dark, blind world, so enlighten us, O God, with Your divine wisdom, which is a co-worker of Your throne. Send down Your wisdom from Your holy heaven and the throne of Your glory, and be with us and work with us, so we may know what is pleasing to You. Without this gift, O God, we cannot please You. For this wisdom, Lord, we also ask in the name of Your beloved Son, Jesus Christ, in whom are hidden all the riches of wisdom and knowledge.*